ALL EVE'S HALLOWS

ALL EVE'S HALLOWS

A CITY KNIGHTS NOVEL

DEAN WESLEY SMITH

A PHOBOS IMPACT BOOK
AN IMPRINT OF PHOBOS BOOKS
NEW YORK

PHOBOS
IMPACT

A Phobos Impact Book
Published by Phobos Books
200 Park Avenue South
New York, NY 10003
www.phobosweb.com

Distributed in the United States by National Book Network, Lanham, Maryland.

Cover by Zuccadesign

The characters and events in this book are fictitious. Any similarity to actual persons, living or dead, is coincidental and not intended by the author.

Library of Congress Cataloging-in-Publication Data

Smith, Dean Wesley.
    All Eve's hallows : a City Knights novel / Dean Wesley Smith.
      p. cm.
    ISBN 0-9720026-6-9 (pbk. : alk. paper)
    1. Halloween—Fiction. 2. Supernatural—Fiction. 3. City and town life—Fiction. I. Title.
    PS3569.M51765A79 2005
    813'.54—dc22

                                                        2005003193

For Kris,
always the magic in my life

Always remember, any advanced magic
can be made to look machine done
with a good fake switch, a simple black box,
and a soft grinding noise.

—Sign on a wall in a City Knights meeting room

ALL EVE'S HALLOWS

CHAPTER ONE

THE UNICORN DIED

They had only been kissing. Sean would swear to that. Actually, he had never kissed a girl before, but he hadn't told his friends that. Yet, somehow, he had ended up kissing Ashley.

He was sure it had been the "yawn move" his friend Jimmy had told him to try. Sit on the couch, pretend to yawn and stretch, end up with an arm around her. Cool move.

And shocking that it had worked. Ashley had to be the biggest prude in the entire tenth grade, yet the minute his arm had gotten around her, she had sighed and leaned back into him and started kissing him.

They were both sunk down real deep into Ashley's mother's big couch. Ashley's mom didn't get home until five, which gave them a good hour every day.

At one point, when they came up for air, Ashley sighed and smiled at him. "You kiss real good for someone who hasn't kissed anyone before."

He started to deny it, lie through his teeth to protect his honor, but she shook her head and put a wonderful, soft finger against his lips to stop him before a word came out.

"I like that about you." Then she went back to kissing him again.

And man, Ashley kissed real nice. And smelled good, too. Like she had just got out of a shower, even though she'd been at school with him all day. She was kissing him real hard, her breath mint bouncing against his teeth, when a loud thud echoed through the apartment's front door.

Ashley sort of levitated away from him, scrambling to her feet and pulling her blouse into position before the thump even stopped echoing.

Sean wiped off his mouth and tried to get his heart to slow down. The street noise from Lexington Avenue filled the apartment as they both stood there, listening.

Someone laughed in the hall, just outside the door. It wasn't like any laugh Sean had ever heard. More like it came from a toy, sort of high and evil-sounding. The laugh sent chills down his spine.

Ashley looked out through the front-door peephole, twisting her head back and forth trying to see something.

Then she shook her head. "Nothing."

"Probably your neighbor," Sean said, hoping that she would come back to the couch and join him again.

Before Ashley could say anything, the high laugh echoed again through the room. Sean shivered. Man, that was downright creepy, like it was outside the door and inside his head at the same time.

Ashley's brown eyes were as wide as Sean had ever seen them. There was no way they were going to get back to kissing until he found out what that was.

He went to the door, peeked out, and saw nothing. The hall looked empty.

He nodded to Ashley, as if he were a real hero about to face down an alien. He reached for the door, but she stopped him, blocking his way. "No."

"Why not?"

"You don't know what's out there."

"And I ain't gonna know if we keep on standin' here," Sean said.

He pushed her aside, unsnapped the lock on the door, and pulled it open.

The last thing he expected to see was a pony lying on the landing in front of Ashley's door. This was Manhattan. He doubted there was a horse outside of Central Park, let alone lying on a third-floor landing.

"Oh, no," Ashley said.

The laugh echoed again, this time from down the stairs. Sean jumped over the pony and looked down the stairs. What looked like a short man, or a thin, tall kid, stood on the next landing down, looking up at Sean. He wore a weird green hat and dance tights.

"It's still a week until Halloween," Sean shouted down the stairs.

The kid grinned at Sean with nasty brown teeth, and then vanished down the stairs, the laugh echoing as he went.

Sean forced his eyes closed, then open again, trying to make sense out of what he had just seen.

"Why would anyone do this?" Ashley asked.

Sean turned to see Ashley sitting on the floor, the pony's head in her lap. Only someone had stuck a horn on this pony's forehead, making it look like a unicorn from a fantasy book. The horn was sharp-looking and had just about every color of the rainbow on it.

Clearly the pony with the glued-on horn was hurt. Blood formed a small pool of bright red, and some ran toward the stairs.

Ashley was slowly petting the pony's head, saying over and over that it was all right. The pony opened its eyes and Sean couldn't believe what he saw. Swirling, bright colors, like rainbows, filled the pony's eyes. It looked at him and he felt immense sadness, so strong his knees almost gave out.

The thing really was a unicorn!

Then it looked up at Ashley and the feeling Sean got was of love.

Then the unicorn sort of flickered, like it wasn't there. It was replaced by Ashley's mother, cradled in Ashley's arms there on the landing.

Then it was the unicorn again.

"No, Mom, no!" Ashley sobbed, burying her face in the pony's neck.

"Stay safe," the unicorn said in a voice that sounded a lot like Ashley's mother's voice. Then the unicorn sort of shuddered, closed its eyes, and died. The colors in its horn faded slowly, like a rainbow drifting off after a storm.

Ashley sobbed into the unicorn's neck as another high, ugly laugh echoed through the building, seeming to come from every wall around them.

Sean had no idea what to do. He'd never imagined anything like this. He wanted more than anything to just run down the stairs and as far away from this building as he could get. But instead he just stood there.

Finally, he managed to say, "I'll call the police."

"No!" Ashley said, staring up at him through her tears.

Behind those tears he thought he caught a glimpse of swirling, rainbow eyes. This was just too weird.

"I'll take care of this," she said. "I know who to call. Just go home."

"But—"

was that the last team of security guards before them had been shot by robbery suspects.

Getting shot wasn't on her night's plan. A burger, yes, a bullet, no.

Another scraping sound to her right, just beyond an empty counter that during the day was covered with watches. Now all that was left was a countdown sign telling her that there were only seven more shopping days until Halloween. She saw movement behind the counter, but couldn't tell if it was just one person or two.

Her com unit clicked once, telling her that Harry was coming down the back stairs and was about to open the security door. Perfect. He would flank the intruder.

She clicked back once to tell Harry to come ahead. Then, with a deep breath, she stood, pointing her gun at the intruder. "Stand real still, now. I'd hate to get too much of your blood on that jewelry case."

A short white guy, young, with a wild look in his dark eyes, turned to face her. He had shaggy black hair and a dark mustache. He was dressed in a Mets sweatshirt and had a screwdriver in his hands.

Her double vision from the head injury showed an even shorter guy superimposed inside the young one, only the vision guy was older, with a full beard and beady, dark eyes. The vision made it look like some sort of troll-creature was controlling the boy.

She ignored the vision and focused on the kid's face.

"Put the screwdriver down," Harry said, moving up from the other side, his gun drawn as well.

"You're screwed enough as it is," Billie said.

The kid glanced at Harry, then back at Billie, and then both images laughed at her. She wasn't sure which laugh she hated the most, the kid's or the hallucination's.

"Nice try," the kid said, his voice low and gruff. The troll's mouth moved with the kid's, as if one were a puppet of a very poor ventriloquist. "But you're not Knights. You can't touch me."

"Oh, we can touch you plenty," Billie said. "Now drop the screwdriver and get on the floor, facedown, hands over your head."

Outside, sirens stopped near the main door. Harry had called New York City's finest to help.

The kid and the troll inside him both shook their heads; then, faster than Billie thought possible, the kid went over the display case and toward the subway entrance.

Harry went one way around the counter, Billie the other, flanking the kid as he tried to escape. Billie had no doubt the kid would fail. The subway was blocked with thick bars. However he had gotten inside, that wasn't the way.

She cut behind a cash register and was only two steps behind the kid when he reached the gate blocking the subway entrance . . .

. . . and went right through.

Not possible!

Yet she had seen it happen.

Not possible!

The kid sort of vanished, leaving the small, troll-like hallucination, which somehow twisted itself right through the bars.

"Stop!" she shouted as the kid and the troll headed down the stairs. "Or I'll shoot!"

Suddenly, it was as if the kid and the hallucination had run into a sticky net. His feet left the ground and he was tossed backward up four stairs to lie on the ground at Billie's feet on the other side of the bars.

"No need to shoot," a deep voice said. "We have him."

With that, two men stepped out of what Billie swore was the concrete stair wall. One man had to be the best-looking creature she had ever seen, hallucination or not.

"Okay," Billie said to herself, blinking to try to make the two men vanish the way they had appeared. "Time to go back to the doctors."

CHAPTER THREE

A GOOD STORY WASTED

Thomas Kenn let the other Knight take care of the troll and turned to the two security guards standing open-mouthed on the Bloomingdale's side of the steel-barred gate. He was going to have a mess taking care of them and the cops outside. Since the guards had called the police, he couldn't just use a simple forget spell. No, he was going to have to plant a new story and make sure it held. And all just to test this woman. What a pain. He sure hoped she would be worth it.

"What just happened here?" the woman demanded, her voice filling the subway staircase. "And where did the two of you come from? Who are you? And what are you going to do with that guy?"

Thomas studied her. She was very nice-looking in a hard sort of way. Actually, better-looking than her picture. Short-chopped brown hair, large brown eyes that didn't seem to miss a detail, and a body that couldn't be over five-three, trim and perfectly proportioned. Thomas figured her for maybe twenty-one at best. He had coats that were twice her age.

Plus, she had magic. He could see it. But did she know she had it, and could she use it? Time to find out.

"Let me tell you what happened," Thomas said, waving his hand in front of both guards to pull them into the story spell he was casting. "A young boy, no more than twelve or so, broke in through the loose bar right here."

Thomas pointed to a low metal bar on the gate. Then, using a simple melting spell, he broke the weld and made the bar drop to the floor. It left a space small enough for a young boy to squeeze through, but neither of the two adult guards.

"You stopped him and he ran, escaping down into the subway."

The older male guard was nodding, taking in the story completely, as would any normal person.

"You want to go tell the police now to call off their alarm?" Thomas said. "That the kid got away."

"I'll do that," the man said, turning and moving toward the front door.

The woman looked after her partner for a moment, then turned back to Thomas. "How did you get Harry to believe that bull? And just what did you do to make that bar fall out? You didn't even touch it."

Thomas stared at the attractive young woman, stunned. His story spell had not caught her. Not even close. Untrained magic, and powerful enough to stop his spell.

"So exactly what did you see?" Thomas asked, keeping his voice level. No one had stopped one of his spells in two hundred years. He didn't much like the idea of someone doing it now.

"I saw that man somehow go through these bars," she said, banging a fist into the metal. "I don't know how he did it, but I saw it. And then you two came out of nowhere and caught him with some sort of net. And to be honest, I'm getting sort of pissed off that you're trying to screw with me. In fact, how do I know you weren't working with the robber? I don't see a badge or uniform."

"You could see our net?" Thomas asked, ignoring the rest of her tirade. It was amazing that she saw it without any training at all. No one but the most powerful could see an entrapment-spell net. It was why they worked so well on petty crooks, and especially well on trolls.

"Of course I could see it," she said, disgusted. "And I'll see how you did it when I watch the security tapes that caught all this."

She pointed to a camera aimed at where they were standing.

He nodded, managing to keep his mind solidly on his task. She was very powerful, of that he had no doubt. And they could use her help. But she was untrained. He was going to have to go slowly, carefully.

"The security tapes will show the boy, and the exact story I told your partner. It will not show us capturing the man or this conversation I am having with you."

"And you can do that exactly *how*?"

"Just call it a little trick," Thomas said. "I'm more interested in the man that you chased, the one we captured. Was there something else about him that you could see as well?"

"Like what?" she asked defensively.

"You tell me," Thomas said, stepping closer to her, the bars of the gate now the only thing between them. "You saw something more in the man you were chasing, didn't you?"

She glanced behind her to make sure her partner wasn't nearby, then turned defiantly to face Thomas. "He

15

looked like a damn troll. There, are you satisfied that I'm nuts?"

He nodded. "I'm satisfied that you are very powerful. Do you have a break coming shortly?"

"Why?"

"There's something we need to talk about. I bet you've been thinking your double visions are a problem, haven't you?"

"Got me kicked out of the Marines," she said. "So I guess you could call them a *problem*."

Her voice, low and mean, told him she was about as angry as he ever wanted to see this powerful woman get. There was no telling what kind of wild magic might come from her.

"Well," Thomas said, smiling at her, doing his best to calm her down. "Your visions are a gift. And if you give me the time it takes for you to take a break from your work, I'll explain what I mean."

"Why should I even listen to you?"

"Because you actually did see a troll," Thomas said. "That's how he got through these bars. Trolls from the old country can get through the smallest spaces. And you could see the net we captured him in. Believe what you see."

"I've been working hard for six months to not believe what I'm seeing. So what can you tell me that a half dozen doctors couldn't?"

"More than you can imagine," Thomas said. "Besides, if you don't let me explain, you're going to spend the rest of your life wondering if you should have."

"Yeah, right," she said. "I spend my nights worrying about conversations I never had with strangers."

He smiled at her. "I can show you how to control the visions so they don't get in your way. If nothing else, you can live a normal life. That has to be worth a little of your time."

"And what's it going to cost me?"

"Nothing but the time," Thomas said. He didn't want to tell her that what it really might cost her was the rest of her life working a job she was born for yet couldn't now imagine.

She stared at him for a long moment, her large brown eyes seeming to hold him in place. He couldn't sense a spell of any type, but with untrained talent like hers, there was no telling. What was very clear was how beautiful she was.

Finally, she nodded. "P. J. Clarke's in twenty minutes. You know where the place is?"

He smiled. "Best cheeseburgers in all the city. I'll be there."

She nodded and started to head to where her partner was bringing in the police.

"One more thing. Back up your partner's story. Trust me on that if nothing else."

Using a walk-through spell, he turned and vanished through the cement-and-stone wall of the building. If she still showed up after seeing him vanish like that, he might just get the honor of bringing in a new recruit.

And then all the problems of sending that troll in there to test her would be worth it.

good-looking man sitting across from her as the hamburgers were delivered. He seemed to actually be there.

The woman in the front booth again touched the unicorn's horn. Billie looked away.

Unicorns, trolls, a man walking through walls. At least the smell and taste of the big, juicy hamburger were real.

She hoped.

CHAPTER FIVE

RESPECT FROM ALL THE WRONG HALLUCINATIONS

Billie wiped some ketchup off her mouth and looked the man who called himself Thomas right in his brown eyes. "I'm not saying I'm believing all this. But tell me about these Sold-ats."

Thomas nodded. "Just say City Knights. It's easier. And I'll answer any question you have about what we do, but first I need to tell you a few things that we have done concerning you."

"Me?" She didn't like the sound of this at all. "You didn't even know my name until we sat down here."

"Oh, I knew it," Thomas said. "In fact, I could tell you the name of everyone in this restaurant."

"Neat trick," she said as she glanced around. No one was paying any attention to their conversation. Typical New Yorkers.

"Since we met, before this little meeting," Thomas said, "I did some fast research on you, your training in the Marines, your foster parents. Right now my boss has a team looking into who your birth parents might be."

"So," she said, "anyone with access to my Marine files could get that much information. And just why would you care about who my birth parents might be?"

"Because you must have had at least one parent with magical ability. From the untrained power I'm seeing coming from you, I'm guessing you had two magical parents. You must have some magical lineage before you can join Soldats de la Fantastiques."

Billie scooted her chair back a few inches, getting ready to stand. "I said nothing about joining your organization. I just asked what it was."

"I know," Thomas said. "But unless there is a chance you might join us, I can't tell you about it. So just humor me and say you are thinking about it. It pays better than your Bloomingdale's job, I can tell you that much."

"All right, I'm thinking about it. But be quick. My dinner break doesn't last all night."

"I understand," Thomas said, nodding. "First, let me tell you there are over a thousand different species of Fantastics. That we know of, that is."

She took another bite. From the way this was going, she was going to be heading back to work a little early.

"The important thing," he said, "is that the treaty stopped what would have been a lot of killing, and allowed the Fantastics to blend in with humans and live in the same world." He pointed to the unicorn man sitting near the front door. "City Knights, men and women like me, keep the peace as best we can."

"Now, I know I saw this in a movie. A bad one."

Thomas's eyes became distant for a moment; then he smiled at her and leaned forward. "You really don't have any idea who your birth parents were, do you?"

"None of your damned business," Billie said. She had spent a month before going into the Marines looking for her real parents, after her scumbag foster parents kicked her out onto the street on her seventeenth birthday. It was a very sore subject for her.

"Well, my boss just told me that we know," Thomas said.

Billie pushed her plate away and stood.

"One hundred and ten thousand a year, U.S. dollars, starting pay," Thomas said, staying seated and picking at a French fry as if what he was saying didn't mean a thing to him. "We furnish you with your own apartment here in the city, and give you a special car, parking for the car, and a clothing budget."

Billie stared down at the man. She clearly was hallucinating now. No one just came out of the blue, talked about her birth parents, and then offered her a job that good.

"Who do I have to kill?"

He laughed. "Hopefully, no one, at least early on."

She sat back down and looked the handsome man directly in the eye, trying to see past his fantastic looks and into his eyes. "Tell me more."

He laid out enough money on the table to pay for both meals, plus a nice tip, then stood. "How about I show you instead. My boss, Ethti, wants to meet you."

She normally wouldn't tag along with a stranger, but she had her gun. She figured she could take care of herself. "How long is this going to take? I don't want to lose the job I have."

"You will be thirty minutes late getting back to your current job if you do not accept our offer. Is that acceptable?"

"I'll call Harry and let him know after we get outside."

Thomas nodded and said nothing.

"What kind of name is Ethti?" she asked as she stood, took one more French fry, then moved to follow Thomas toward the front door.

"A very old name. She's over a thousand years old."

Right. Of course.

The unicorn man near the door glanced up at Thomas. The human part didn't seem to notice, but the unicorn part nodded at Thomas. Then the unicorn glanced at her with its big, round eyes, and nodded to her as well.

"My hallucinations are paying attention to me now," Billie said as she and Thomas stepped onto the sidewalk and turned north, back toward Bloomingdale's.

"All Fantastics can see City Knights," Thomas said. "It's an aura our magic gives off. Humans are rarely magical in nature. That is why trying to recruit you into our ranks is worth so much of my time."

"Thanks," she said, disgusted at his attitude. "I hope I'm not keeping you from more *important* matters."

"Actually, you are," Thomas said, raising an arm for a cab. "But that's beside the point."

Chapter Six

TAN LINES OF EVIL

"**A**wake!"

The word echoed and then died off the cold stone walls around Eve. She remained poised, her hand above her head, her index finger pointed at the stone roof of her secret chamber two hundred feet below the city of New York.

Around her feet, the complex diagram remained, etched in the stone with the blood of a dozen unicorns. It had taken her six days to draw the stupid thing, not counting all the time it had taken to find, kill, and drain unicorns.

What a pain. And what a mess. But it would be worth it, if this worked.

Eve tried to hold her breath, but found that hard in the tight-fitting black dress she had thought appropriate for siphoning off power from an ancient, evil horror.

She lowered her arm, chanted two more words, then shouted once again. "Awake, O Mighty One!"

Again, for the drama of it—and for her assistant, who was recording the entire grand event—she thrust her arm upward at the ceiling.

There was a slight cloth-ripping sound from under her arm, but otherwise nothing happened.

She was supposed to start feeling the power of the great creature who lay slumbering below her. Four years ago, she had discovered the presence of Rallidae, the ancient Bird King. Far below the city, in an ancient hallows, it slept, nothing but a huge blob of pure evil, guarded by thousands of evil sprites also called hallows, all trapped together in a huge chamber a hundred miles below the surface.

Some great power had trapped it there, putting it to sleep long before Fantastics and humans began to fight. Her destiny was to take Rallidae's power and use it to control the world for herself.

"Oh, come on," she muttered. "I know this has to work." Her feet hurt and her back ached from holding the pose.

"Is it a-happenin'?" Snake Boy asked.

Actually, his name was Steve, and he was from Brooklyn, but since her name was Eve, she thought it only fitting that her assistant should be a snake. So she had called him Snake Boy, and he had loved it, going so far as to tattoo a snake on his neck. Actually, it looked more like a worm, but she wasn't saying anything.

"It's going to take time," she said.

She lowered her arms and then started to step away from the center of the diagram. Suddenly a black funnel of nothingness came up out of the floor right where she had been standing.

The big, swirling mass shot up into the ceiling and beyond.

She stepped back into the center of the funnel before too much of the energy could escape.

"Fill me!" she shouted, thrusting both arms into the air. It wasn't part of the power spell that was draining the ancient king, but it would look good on the film.

She could feel the energy flowing through her as the great being below her slowly woke up enough for her to drain some of its vast power.

It felt wonderful.

—Like swimming in a black lake on a dark night.

—Like washing her face in crude oil.

—Like feeling the sugar rush of a large package of Oreo cookies.

This was what you would call a real "power bath."

In the swirling blackness that went past her, she could see the bright-eyed images of hallows, also released by her spell. They had been guarding the huge black body of Rallidae for centuries. Now she was releasing the spritelike evil creatures into the city of New York.

The destruction they would cause would be minor compared with what she would do when she gained all Rallidae's strength and rose to take over the world. She would rule everything.

She laughed and let the energy flow into her soul, through every pore of her skin, up her skirt like a wind from a subway grate.

"Time!" she heard Snake Boy say, seemingly from a distance. He had been instructed to make sure she didn't stay in the power too long at first. It might be too much for her to handle. She needed to be careful, soak in the blackness a little bit at a time.

She took as large a breath as she could in the tight dress, then waved both hands over her head and shouted, "Enough!"

For a moment, she wasn't sure if her command had shut down the energy coming from the slowly waking evil. Then the column of blackness faded as one last hallow went through the ceiling and up into the city.

"Mistress!" Snake Boy said, jumping to her side as she slumped onto the now-faded diagram. "Are you all right? Are you all right?"

"Of course I am," she said, brushing him aside like a leaf blowing in the wind. "I feel more powerful than ever. It worked, you fool. It worked."

Snake Boy staggered back, not taking his eyes off her.

"What?" she asked, standing, enjoying the feel of the new power that coursed through her. "What?"

She glanced down at her body, thinking that maybe her dress had ripped and she was giving Snake Boy a good shot of sorceress boob.

"Oh, my," she said, studying her arms. Her once pure white skin had turned dark and very shiny, as if she had been dipped in a bucket of enamel paint. She rubbed her arm with a black hand, but none of it came off that she could tell.

"Beautiful, isn't it?"

Snake Boy gulped and nodded.

"Just think. When I rule the world, I will be known as Eve, the Dark Sorceress. Nice."

Then she moved and caught a glimpse of white skin down the front of her low-cut dress. She pulled the strap aside to see all-white skin under the strap.

"What is this?" She pulled off her dress, to the gasp of Snake Boy. It seemed that only her exposed skin had been turned dark by the energy from Rallidae.

She laughed, the sound echoing powerfully in the stone chamber. Tomorrow, when she opened the stream of energy again, she would step into the power completely nude.

After all, it wouldn't do for a dark sorceress to be seen with tan lines.

CHAPTER SEVEN

AN OATMEAL ADVENTURE

"**H**ere," Thomas said to the cabdriver.

The driver pulled half out of the lane and stopped, right across from the Seventy-ninth Street entrance to Central Park. Billie glanced at her watch. She had exactly twenty minutes left on her break, and a chunk of that time was going to be eaten up getting back to Bloomingdale's.

Thomas overpaid for the cab ride and got out, motioning for her to follow him across the street and into the park.

Sometimes she thought her foster mother had been right when she had told Billie she had oatmeal for brains. This was an oatmeal situation, that was for sure.

Thomas hadn't said a word to her since they had climbed into the cab. Now he just strode up East Drive, moving toward the Metropolitan Museum of Art, which she was sure had been closed for hours.

Just past the museum, Thomas moved across the street and toward Cleopatra's Needle, the ancient obelisk that someone had once told her was the twin for one in London. Supposedly, it dated from 1600 B.C. Even though she had lived in the city most of her life, she had no idea why it was in the park, or what it symbolized.

"Stay close," he said, glancing at her.

Then, suddenly, a door in front of him appeared in the air, as if there were a huge, invisible building around the Needle. Six stone steps went up to the door, steps that hadn't been there a moment before.

For the first time since meeting this guy, she started to believe he was real. And that thought scared the hell out of her.

He went up the stairs and through the open door that seemed to hang in the air. Clearly he expected her to follow.

Which she did. She didn't have oatmeal for brains. Oatmeal was smarter than this.

Around them a good dozen people were on the street and sidewalk, and who knew how many others in the bushes. "Aren't all these other people going to see your secret door?"

"Only humans with magic can see it," Thomas said without looking around.

As she stepped through the door, the noise of the street and the lights in the park just vanished, as if she had actually stepped inside a building.

And then the door, the park, the street, the big ugly Needle vanished as well.

"Hey!" she said. Thomas paid no attention, and like an idiot she kept following him.

The walls around her were made of some sort of dark rock, like parts of the subway in the old sections. The same kind of rock that many of the oldest buildings in the city were made of.

Ten paces and they entered a large, round room, with a good dozen tunnels heading off in all directions like spokes on a wheel. Dome-shaped, the room was also made of the stone, and each tunnel had a stone arch over it. No signs anywhere, nothing to tell which tunnel went where.

She glanced back. They had come out of one of those spokes, underneath one stone arch, but for the life of her she couldn't see anything back down the tunnel. She thought of making a mark on the tunnel entrance. She would have dropped bread crumbs if she had any.

"Where are we?"

"North American headquarters for Soldats de la Fantastiques," Thomas said.

"Seems kind of deserted," she said, her hand firmly on the butt of her gun. Somehow, this creep had managed to lead her into a subway tunnel of some sort. If he tried anything, he would quickly learn what it was like to tangle with a United States marine.

"Every tunnel leads to a different part of the continent. This is only one of the many ways in and out of the headquarters. It was simply the closest to where we were."

He stopped in the middle of the stone floor, right under the tallest part of the dome, and waited for her to come closer.

"Security precautions," he said. "We don't want any Fantastics getting in here that don't belong."

Suddenly, they were dropping down a stone shaft. The entire center of the room was some sort of elevator. For the second time in the last five minutes, she believed that this guy might be what he said he was.

Either that, or someone had slipped some pretty weird drugs in her coffee.

The stone elevator dropped through the ceiling of a huge cave, seemingly floating in the air. The cave was large enough to fit Yankee Stadium and tall enough to not bend any of the light towers.

From what she could see as they drifted downward, the huge cave was functioning like a giant office, with cubicles filling most of the middle of the space, and glass-walled offices along the rock walls. There were hundreds and hundreds of people below, and none of them seemed to notice the big rock slab she stood on.

It looked and sounded like a large office building. People talking, others typing, most moving down paths between cubicles, acting busy. Only this huge office was in a cave instead of a high-rise building.

Big damn difference.

The rock elevator sort of drifted to the right and settled gently in an open area surrounded by coffee machines, a large copier, and a dozen couches. A young couple sat earnestly talking on one couch and didn't seem to notice them.

The slab settled into the rock floor where a moment before there hadn't been a hole.

Thomas moved off to the right and she followed him, glancing back at the elevator platform, expecting it to go back up through one of the many holes in the roof. She couldn't even see where it was anymore.

"Wow, some ride. What is this place?"

"I told you," Thomas said without glancing back at her. "Headquarters."

"And all these people are knights in your organization."

Thomas laughed without turning around. "Hardly. There are one hundred and eleven City Knights and forty-seven squires, basically knights-in-training."

He led her down a wide, carpeted hallway toward one wall of glass offices. Every cubicle seemed to have someone working in it, even at this time of night. The farther they walked, the more she revised up her estimate of how many people were in the huge room.

"So what do all the rest of these people do?" she asked, nodding to a few people who glanced up from their desks as they passed.

Thomas glanced around, then shrugged. "Paper-work."

CHAPTER EIGHT

NO TYPING, JUST KILLING

Thomas finally led Billie into a huge office tucked against one side of the giant cave. The office had a warm feeling, even with one wall of rock and a second wall of glass. Tan, lush carpet covered the floor, a large antique oak desk sat off to one side, with three chairs in front of it. Two leather couches and an overstuffed chair filled another area of the office, forming a small living-room-like space.

The flat wall on the right was covered with oil paintings of Native Americans, and the flat wall on the left was filled with oak bookshelves stuffed with books and Native American artifacts.

Two closed doors led into the rock wall.

"Nice office."

He laughed. "Mine is a couple down on the right. This is Ethti's office."

"Et-ti?" Billie asked, slowly moving around the room, looking at the paintings.

"Eth-ti," a woman said, coming into the room from one of the closed doors. "It is an old tribal name."

Billie turned and just stared. Ethti had the look of a princess, with long flowing hair, a tiny frame, and wide, brown eyes. She had on the tightest-fitting jeans Billie had ever seen, and a silk blouse that left nothing to the imagination.

"I assume you are the Billie that Thomas reported to me," Ethti said, seeming to float forward, hand extended.

"Billie Stein." She was careful to not shake Ethti's tiny hand too tightly. It felt like she was shaking hands with a baby bird. There was almost nothing to Ethti's touch beyond a sense of warmth.

Ethti stared at Billie for a moment, her large eyes getting wider and wider.

Billie felt herself drawn into the eyes, tipping toward them. She forced herself to stay solidly planted on her feet, centered. The warmth coming from Ethti's hand grew into heat as the pull toward the frail woman increased.

Finally, Ethti nodded and turned away, letting go of Billie's hand. The release of pressure was so much that Billie staggered backward a few steps.

"You were right, Thomas. She has deep power."

"My mother always said I was full of surprises," Billie said, trying to shake the feeling that she had just been tested in some weird way.

"You never knew your mother," Ethti said as she floated around her desk and sat in her chair, indicating that Thomas and Billie should take two of the chairs facing her.

Billie felt like just leaving after that rude comment, but a glance through the glass-walled window told her that a graceful escape wasn't going to be easy. "My foster mother was good enough for me."

"I would suppose she was, child," Ethti said.

Billie bit back another response and just sat down, surprised at how the tiny woman seemed to dominate the room, even across the big desk.

"Please give me a moment to start from the beginning. My name is Ethti, no first or last, just Ethti. I run this entire section of the Soldats de la Fantastiques—City Knights. I was born in the New Orleans area just over a thousand years ago. I am a sorceress."

"You've aged nicely," Billie said, doing her best to not snort out a laugh. Somehow, she managed only a smirk.

"Thank you," Ethti said. "You, Billie Stein, were born twenty years ago to a sorceress named Bell and a powerful magician and City Knight named Danny Boy."

"Oh, no wonder," Thomas said, shaking his head.

"Yes," Ethti said, also shaking her head. "No wonder."

Billie looked at him, then at the tiny woman across the desk; then she stood, defiantly facing the tiny woman. "Look, I'm getting tired of this stupid joke. I don't have any money, nothing for you people to rob, so just release me from this hypnotic trance or whatever you're doing to me, and let me go back to work. I'm going to be late as it is."

"Sit down," Ethti said.

Billie suddenly had a huge desire to sit down, but remained standing anyway.

"Very powerful," Ethti said, nodding at Thomas. "And stubborn as well."

The desire to sit down left.

Ethti looked at Billie directly. "Please, just give me a few more moments of your time."

Billie glanced at the wall of glass and all the cubicles and people working on the other side of it, then nodded and sat back down.

"We can talk more about your real parents later," Ethti said. "I will explain why you were put up for adoption and lost to our records as best I can."

"Sounds like a real joyride," Billie said.

Ethti ignored the snide comment and went on. "Thomas tells me you are working at Bloomingdale's as a night security guard. Is that correct?"

"I was. But that might end if I get back too late from this little meeting."

"I would like to offer you a job so that you don't have to go back."

"So he said." She jerked her thumb toward Thomas. "But it looks like you've got the wrong gal. I don't do paperwork. That's why I joined the Marines. No typing, just killing."

Ethti smiled. "No typing, I promise. And with luck, not much killing."

"Not much?" Billie asked. "How much is not much?"

"Only when it is needed, and very seldom on other humans."

"But it does happen," Thomas said.

"Yes, it does," Ethti said.

"Oh." Billie didn't much like where this was going.

"Your starting salary would be two hundred thousand U.S. dollars a year. . . ."

"Two hundred thousand?" Billie asked. She glanced at Thomas. "You said less than that."

"Of course I did," he said. "You wouldn't have believed me otherwise."

Billie had to admit he was right. She wouldn't have.

"So what is this job, exactly?"

"You would become a squire, a City Knight in training. Your job would be to help keep the peace between the Fantastics and the humans they live among. And to be honest, with an outbreak of ancient hallows around this city, we could use your help, starting tonight. This group seems to be of a species we haven't seen before."

"Tonight?"

Ethti nodded. "We have a way of giving you your first training very quickly. Of course, you will have to do other training sessions each week."

"Of course."

"When you prove yourself, you will become a full City Knight, with all the benefits and privileges that go with that duty. But that will take some time."

Billie glanced around. These people had money. A lot of money. And she would much rather believe that the double-vision problem had a reason instead of just being a head injury.

Besides, the job at Bloomingdale's didn't much matter anyway. She could get another. She really didn't have much to lose by taking this offer and riding it out, seeing just what was really going on.

She looked at Thomas and then at Ethti. "I still think you two are nuts, or I've gone completely nuts."

"Possibly both," Thomas said.

"Encouraging," Billie said.

"Will you take what has been offered?" Ethti asked.

"Sure, why not? If I become a knight, do I get to joust?"

Ethti looked at Billie with a puzzled and serious expression on her face. "If you would like to ride a horse, and run others through with a long stick, I think it could be arranged."

"Uh, no, thanks," Billie said. "It was just a joke."

"Oh," Ethti said, staring at Billie. "I think I have heard of such things."

Then slowly, she smiled, and Billie knew she had been had.

CHAPTER NINE

LAUGH NIGHT; OR, I KILLED A UNICORN

"Must you be so slow?" Eve growled in the direction of her assistant, Snake Boy, who was lagging behind in their climb up to street level. Old stone stairs were the only way out of her secret hideaway. The stairs, covered in sewage and moss, were slick and damp and steep.

She floated above them, seldom having to even touch her hand to the wall. Snake Boy, having no powers of levitation, or even good balance for that matter, had fallen twice, once bouncing down ten steps before stopping. Now he limped and was even slower than before. But she couldn't go on without him. She needed him for the bleeding ritual.

When she had all the power of Rallidae, she had decided, she would live in a penthouse, not in a cave. She would rule the world from the light of day, high in the sky, her dark skin taking in the energy.

And she would have an elevator.

Just the thought made her giddy.

But for the next number of days, she needed to remain in the underground chamber, sucking up the power, getting ready to ascend to her rightful place. That day would come soon.

Except for the tan lines, the first big suck had gone according to plan. But for tomorrow night she needed the blood of another unicorn to replenish the diagram etched into the stone floor.

She finally reached the entrance that led into a lower subway tunnel. She removed the power-blocking screen she had set up to hide the opening, then floated out into the trash-and-diesel smell of the subway tunnel. She started down the tunnel toward the closest platform, letting Snake Boy limp along behind her as best he could.

She had made sure that the first six unicorns she killed and drained were scattered around the different boroughs. So it didn't matter that this one was close to where she worked. She had left no pattern in her harvest, and the damn Knights couldn't protect all four hundred and sixty-three remaining unicorns in the metropolitan area.

She levitated herself up onto the subway platform. When Snake Boy climbed onto the platform, she took him by his right ear and lifted him off the ground, holding him in a very painful way. She knew he loved it.

"Do you know what we're going to do?"

"Yes, O beautiful dark one," he said, his eyes growing distant from the pain.

"Good," she said, dropping him back onto the concrete. "Get up to the street and get us a cab."

He scrambled away from her, half-limping, half-running toward the stairs.

She followed along slowly, taking her time, enjoying the thought of the coming event. Draining unicorns was always so much fun. Of course, she had to be careful to not touch any of the pure blood. It would eat into her perfect dark skin like acid. But she always loved watching the unicorn's look of disbelief, right up to the moment of death. So trusting. Saps.

She especially liked Snake Boy's laugh when they drained one. He couldn't do it while helping her bathe, or while making her dinner, or while begging for his own dinner like a dog. His evil cackle was reserved only for the draining ritual. Maybe, after she had taken over the world, she would round up the unicorns and put them all in a giant pen. Then, once a week, she would have one brought out and drained just for Snake Boy.

She would call the event Laugh Night, and broadcast the sound to what was left of the world. It would strike fear into anyone trying to oppose her.

Of course, no one would be stupid enough, or alive enough, to try that by then, but it was still a good reason for Laugh Night.

CHAPTER TEN

NOT DRESSED
FOR FREEDOM

Man, it felt good to be free again.

Pool sat on a stone ledge on a building, twenty body lengths in the air, staring down at the night and all the strange machines and humans passing by his perch. It seemed so odd, so wrong, that humans filled up everything. And even stranger that Fantastics used fake human skins to hide in.

In the last forty thousand, one hundred and seven years, something had gone very wrong.

Pool had been trapped that long with that snoring, smelly mess, that giant mound of evil jelly, that sleeping blob of nastiness called Rallidae. Pool and six thousand, two hundred and eleven of his brother hallows had been trapped by the forces of good in that deep hole.

Led by the Great King of all the unicorns, those so-called Pure and Clean Ones defeated Rallidae, the Great Bird King, in an epic battle that had been so much fun,

Pool still remembered every detail. Fun, that is, until Rallidae lost. The Pure and Clean Ones had sentenced Rallidae to spend all eternity sleeping in a cave under a massive rock on a distant continent. For the small and insignificant act of taking Rallidae's side in the final battle, the sprites trapped with him had been changed to hallows, doomed to live forever, doing nothing but watching the old mess sleep.

Boring.

No, boring didn't begin to describe what he had been through over all those years. There was no word for what he had experienced. There had been no one to play tricks on, no human cattle to torment, no fairies to chase through the trees. Just pixies and a few elves, all changed into hallows to protect the hallows confinement area, living in darkness.

And that didn't even take into account the smell. Horse piss combined with rotted meat combined with six-day-old dead fish would have smelled better than Rallidae.

Torture. It had been pure, immortal torture.

The only excitement happened when Rallidae turned over in his sleep.

Two or three centuries ago, Rallidae had rolled over and passed gas at the same time. Pool's eyes had watered for years after, and seven hallows had died.

He had never thought the imprisonment would end, right up to the moment that the human woman in the fancy gown started to wake the big guy up.

Free. A mere human had set him free.

Coming back to the surface had been a shock. When Rallidae got himself trapped by the other side and put into the long nap, the planet had been ruled by trolls and policed by fairies. Humans, magicless and stupid, hunted in small bands and mostly occupied a side continent, not bothering anyone. They had been an amusement, dumb animals the sprites and elves loved to pick on. The trolls and fairies had never really cared what the sprites did to humans, as long as only humans were targets.

It was quite a surprise, coming to the surface and finding all the Fantastic clans walking around in phony human bodies, acting human, pretending to be human, seeming perfectly happy. Even elves and pixies and other sprites, clearly of his old clan's lineage, had taken on human form.

Shocking.

A few humans even had magic powers. Some magical creature must have decided, at some point after Rallidae started his nap, that humans looked attractive enough to have relations with.

Intimate kinds of relations.

The very thought of it made Pool shudder so much that he almost fell off his rock ledge. But it must have happened, and thus magic was passed to some of the offspring and carried down through generations.

On top of all that, the humans had gotten a lot taller. Pool barely came up to a human's midsection now. What in the world had they been eating to become such giants?

But tall or short, they were still going to be fun to torment. Below him, a young couple strolled arm-in-arm. Pool went invisible, then scampered down the wall and came up behind the couple, using a long nail on his finger to tickle the woman's bare leg.

She slapped at his hand and kept walking, as if he were nothing more than a bug.

The male waved his hand in front of his face. "Wow, something's rotten around here."

The girl held her nose. "You're not kidding."

He had started to reach for her leg again when a net dropped over him.

He moved to rip the net off, but it was magically enhanced and very strong.

"Where did you come from?" a human voice asked in perfect Fantastic language. "And when was the last time you had a bath?"

The human seemed to have strong magical powers. It could see the hallow, even through the invisible spell Pool cast.

"Who are you, human?" Pool demanded. "And what gives you the right to stop and capture me?"

The human male looked at Pool for a moment, then actually had the audacity to laugh. "The Great Treaty gives me the right. I am a City Knight."

With that, the human snapped up the ends of the net, closing it around Pool's feet. As if picking up a sack of grain, the human slung Pool into the back of a nearby machine and slammed a lid. Suddenly Pool was back in the darkness, just as he had been for centuries, his freedom gone.

He kicked and shouted as hard as he could, but the magic net contained him easily.

He couldn't believe it. He was trapped again by some force of good. Only this time, it was a human who had trapped him, not a unicorn army.

How humiliating.

CHAPTER ELEVEN

LEARNED THAT LESSON

"You're going to do *what* to me?" Billie asked Ethti as they walked into a pure white room. It was so *completely* white on the floor, ceiling, and walls that Billie couldn't see the corners, making it feel as if she'd walked out into empty space. No light fixtures, no furniture, nothing. The white paint glowed, giving the room its light.

"We're going to teach you Fantastic," Ethti said as she pulled the white door closed. There was a sucking sound. The seams around the door vanished. Billie couldn't even see where the door had been.

Pure white, all around her. Even Ethti's clothing seemed to be fading to white as Billie watched. It was enough to drive any New Yorker completely bonkers. White just wasn't a New York kind of color.

"We're also going to teach you how to control your magic, give you an understanding of your power, and teach you a few thousand basic spells that will come in handy on your job, either tonight or in the future."

Ethti pointed to a small red dot on the floor in the middle of the pure white room. "Stand there."

Before Billie could ask another question, Ethti seemed to just vanish.

"Hey!"

"Stand on the red dot." A male voice echoed through the white chamber, the force of the command so intense that Billie just moved to the red dot without thinking about it.

Suddenly the white room turned dark. An opaque, thick, cold kind of dark, the kind that swallowed you whole.

Billie felt her skin crawl, her hair blow, and her stomach clamp down into a lump.

Then, quicker than she could blink, the lights came back on, the door opened in the white wall, and Ethti and Thomas strode into the white room, both smiling, leaving the door open behind them like a dark hole into a perfect world.

"How do you feel?" Ethti asked.

"About what?" The moment those two words left her mouth, she knew what Ethti was asking. She understood the history of the City Knights, understood that she was standing in a room that magically placed knowledge in her mind. She knew her own magic, how to control it, how to use it in many ways. She knew exactly what spell Thomas had used to capture the troll who had been trying to steal from Bloomingdale's.

She didn't believe she knew all that stuff.

But she still knew it.

Her head hurt. A splitting headache that suddenly made the entire room spin around her. What had they done to her?

Ethti took her by the arm and led her out, letting Billie drop down onto a chair against a wall facing into the big cave.

"We will go slowly," Ethti said.

"Slow, like cramming-a-ton-of-information-into-my-head-in-a-few-seconds slow?" Billie asked, holding her head and trying to take deep breaths. She was sure that at any moment she was going to wake up back in the military hospital, or in Bloomingdale's, and all this would have been just another of her hallucinations.

"Slow, like not letting you get killed on your first night of duty," Thomas said.

"She will go with you," Ethti said to Thomas. "She needs your guidance. Make sure she gets it."

Billie watched as Thomas started to say something, but Ethti put her hand up, stopping his words in his mouth. Somehow, Billie knew that Ethti had used a silencing spell on Thomas, and was powerful enough to make it stick for the moment.

Billie also knew that it would take Thomas only a few seconds to break the spell. Again, she had no idea how she knew. She just wished her head would stop hurting so much.

She tried to focus, staring at just one woman sitting in a cubicle twenty feet away. Now, after the white room, Billie knew what most of the people in the cubicles did, and why they were needed.

All of them believed they were working a late shift in a high-rise. The deception spell was so old and so well implanted in the cave that Billie could see parts of it hovering in the air like a shadow. In the deception, it looked like a nice place to work. Better than a cave. In the deception, every cubicle had its own window. In New York, if you got a window in your office, you were doing well, so all these people thought they were on the way up. Neat trick.

She tried to push the headache back and take inventory of what she knew. They had gotten everything into her head so easily with a very powerful spell. It was amazing she only had a headache.

"This has to be a dream," she said, shaking her head and instantly regretting it.

For the first time since she bumped her head in Iraq, she understood her double visions. The bump had simply triggered part of her magic, allowing her to see the Fantastics in human disguises.

She also knew who her real father was. And who her real mother was. And that both were dead, killed by a rampaging and insane goblin on a salt-free diet right after she had been born. Nice of Ethti to shove that information in as well. She could see her parents' images in her mind, as if it were a memory.

No grief, just snapshots of memory of two people she would never get to know. It would have been nice if the learning room had implanted a little grief at their loss as well.

CHAPTER TWELVE

TEMPER THIS, JERK FACE

Thomas snapped his fingers in front of Billie as he walked past her. "Big meeting. Follow me and keep your mouth shut."

Billie stood slowly, saluted at the back of Thomas's head, and fell in behind him, headed across the large room between cubicles. Her headache was fading fast, but she still had a nagging worry she was going to wake up in a military hospital.

"We don't salute in the City Knights, *Squire*."

"You saw that?"

"Check in with your magic knowledge. You should be able to see everything around you."

The moment Thomas said that, Billie knew that was possible. She just hadn't realized her magic could do that yet. She blinked, focusing to turn on the three-hundred-and-sixty-degree vision . . .

. . . and fell flat on her face in the aisle.

Thomas must have heard the smack as she hit the floor. He turned around. She was so disoriented that she didn't actually realize she had hit the floor until the pain shot up through her arms.

Two people in nearby cubicles peered out at her, and even though she was lying facedown on the carpet, not looking at them, she could see them.

"Don't you have work to do?" Thomas snapped at the gawkers, who instantly yanked their heads back into their cubicles. Then Thomas reached down, grabbed her arm, and yanked her to her feet.

"Close your eyes. Turn off your full vision."

She snapped her eyes shut, which helped. It took a moment of concentration for her to find her vision controls in all the memories and spells she had been given. She focused on shutting off full vision, then opened her eyes again slowly.

What a relief. She could only see forward. The experience had been like a bad Cinemax experience, and she realized that her dinner was threatening to make a rebirth into the world. Besides that, her elbow hurt.

"We will practice some of your new skills later, Squire," Thomas said, clearly disgusted. "Or you can do them at home, in the safety of your new, magic-guarded apartment. But for now don't try any spells. Understood?"

She nodded, and her stomach was sorry she did.

Thomas turned and kept going across the big room, heading toward a large glassed-in area on the far side. She followed, staying close. She was about to ask him where they were going; then she realized she knew. Big meetings were held in what everyone called the Big Meeting Room, a glassed-in area carved out of the wall on one side of the cave. The room could hold up to a hundred City Knights.

It was damn weird knowing information like that with no memory of reading it from a book or anyone telling it to her. She didn't know which information spinning around in her head to trust and which to not trust.

She did know that a big meeting meant that something was very wrong, or at least she thought that was what it meant.

Suddenly, she realized that she had never called Bloomingdale's and told them she wasn't coming back. "I need to quit my old job."

"Done for you," Thomas said. "While you were in the training room. They know you won't be back."

That made her a little mad. It had been her job, her responsibility to quit.

Two other people, one man, one woman, both dressed in New York evening casual, dropped into step with them. Both looked young, very fit, and very handsome. Actually, now that she thought about it, every City Knight and person she saw working here was fit and good-looking.

The knowledge surfaced that having magic seemed to go with good looks in humans. No one knew why, and she sure didn't. And she sure didn't consider herself good-looking.

She also knew that the man's name was Austin and the woman was Clovie. Somehow, she knew the faces and names of every City Knight and squire working in this area of the world.

"New squire?" Clovie asked Thomas.

"Trained a few minutes ago," Thomas said.

Austin glanced back at Billie and smiled. "Oh, raw magic in such a small package. This could be fun."

Then he winked at her.

Billie felt sudden anger at all the male chauvinist pigs she had ever known, represented now by one man.

Anger at her sergeant in boot, anger at some of the male soldiers in her unit who thought that because she was short she couldn't fight. She was a marine. She could fight.

"You want fun?" Billie asked.

She reached for Austin, with the intention of tossing him over her head and letting him roll like a bowling ball down the wide aisle behind them.

Her hand hit a shield a half foot from his body and stopped.

Thomas shook his head without turning around and they all kept walking.

"Nice temper, sweet thing," Austin said, again winking at her.

This time she went to punch him. Her hand hit something solid about twelve inches from the sneering face, and the jerk laughed harder.

No one laughed at a marine.

Billie knew what her hand had hit because of her new knowledge, what magic the jerk had used. She had no idea how to get through it, so she just did what any good marine would do.

She swung harder.

Her fist hit the jerk's shield again, only this time the shield cracked. Suddenly around the jerk was a ball of what looked like cracked glass, like a rear windshield made of safety glass after being hit with a hammer.

He stopped and grabbed his head, as if her punch had given him a nasty headache.

Billie's fist hurt, but it was worth it.

Clovie stopped, stunned, staring at her partner and his cracked shield.

Thomas just shook his head again and kept walking. "Stay with me, partner. And try not to hit anyone else, would you."

She fell into step beside him. "Sorry. The moron deserved it."

Thomas smiled at her. "Yes, he did. But you're a squire. Try to remember your place."

"I will," she said, remembering her early days in the Marines and the hazing she got then.

Billie glanced behind her. Austin's magic shield seemed to be re-forming, the cracks going away. But he didn't look happy.

Not a good way to win new friends in her new job. She was off to her usual bad start.

And her head hurt again.

CHAPTER THIRTEEN

BASIC MATH, BASIC MAGIC

Billie followed Thomas into the Big Meeting Room, not letting herself glance over her shoulder at Austin, and wishing she had the all-around-vision thing working. Over sixty people were already seated. Ethti and two others were standing near the front on a raised platform.

Thomas pointed at two open chairs near the far side of the room and led the way, getting seated just as Ethti started talking. Austin and Clovie came in a few moments later and sat in the back. Austin glared at her and Billie tried not to smile.

"We have a new and *major* threat," Ethti said.

Billie shuddered. Just the way the woman spoke made Billie respect her, and hope to never cross her.

Two City Knights, both good-looking men about Billie's age, appeared beside Ethti on the main stage, holding a dirty and very short creature between them. Billie had no new training on how they, or Ethti, did the appearing and disappearing act. More than likely it was

Ethti's powers, but Billie wasn't sure why she thought that.

"A hallow," Ethti said, nodding at the creature.

The word sort of triggered a card-catalogue effect in Billie's mind, with details Billie didn't really want to know about hallows flashing through her thoughts.

The sprite came up to the two Knights' belts, and struggled like a pit bull trying to get loose. Billie forced herself to not look at the hallow's crotch. Among the nuggets of intel crammed into her head was a rumor about the generous endowments of the hallows.

She tried not to look, but eventually she couldn't help herself.

Oh, my.

The rumor was true.

Ethti pointed at the hallow. "He is the sixth we have captured in the last ten hours. They are old Fantastics, from before the time of the treaty, new to human culture and the ways of the agreement with humans."

"What rock have they been hiding under?" someone up front asked.

"This rock, actually," Ethti said. "About a hundred miles down, from what we can tell from reading their stunted minds. They have lived there, in prison with an ancient evil called Rallidae from before recorded time. The ancient evil, along with a few thousand sprites like this one, was imprisoned there by the Last Great Unicorn King and his army."

A hush went through the room. Then hands were raised and Ethti was peppered with questions: Who was this Rallidae? How did his minions escape?

Billie knew basic history of the City Knights, but nowhere in her new memories was there anything about a Unicorn King. Maybe that was scheduled in next week's lesson. But she didn't much like the idea that there may be thousands of those naked things running loose.

"A dark energy stream pulled a number of the sprites from the cave," Ethti said. She stood calmly, her hands behind her back, as if talking to a room full of students. "From what we can tell, from the memories of these hallows, a human woman stood in the dark energy stream as they passed to the surface."

"A sorceress?" someone asked.

"So it seems," Ethti said. "She was absorbing the black energy."

"Eve," Thomas said softly to himself.

Billie had no memory of any villain named Eve. But she did have a few other bad-guy images in her mind. The card catalogue of information clicked into action again and she suddenly knew *a lot* about a number of creatures wanted by the City Knights. For example, she knew that Cassius the Epileptic Satyr still plagued the Bronx area, and had led gangs of imps at times over the past two years. Up until today, he had been the local City Knights' most-wanted fugitive.

Thomas's jaw was still clenched tight, and his eyes were still narrowed with—what? Determination? Hatred? Whatever she was reading on her partner's face, Billie didn't need magic to tell her that Thomas and Eve had a history.

"We do know that, once freed, Rallidae and the hallows have enough power to destroy this entire city," Ethti said.

Now, that got everyone's attention.

Ethti let what she had said sink in. Finally, the wall behind her shimmered into a detailed map of the New York metropolitan area. About fifty red dots glowed brightly from the map. All were in Manhattan. Some even near Bloomingdale's and Billie's apartment. The closer Billie looked, the more it appeared that one of them was actually in Bloomingdale's.

"These are the locations of the remaining hallows. They must be captured by first light, their tracks covered. Everyone knows which hallow to go after."

Thomas nodded. Billie had no idea which one they were going after. Clearly her training didn't include the special link to get assignments.

With that, Ethti faded and vanished.

"Nice disappearing act," Billie said, standing as everyone else did.

"She's the most powerful sorceress who has lived in the last century," Thomas said.

On the other side of the room, Austin glared at Billie. She smiled at him and waved. He just turned away, stomping out of the room.

"You think I made him mad?" Billie asked, smiling at Thomas.

"I don't think he's going to bother you again."

"So where are we going?" she asked as they headed for one of the lifts taking Knights toward the ceiling of the big room.

"Bloomingdale's."

"So we can use my real-world knowledge of the layout of the store to help us?"

"Of course not," Thomas said, shaking his head as the lift flashed into the roof of the cave wall and stopped in the same open room with all the tunnels they had been in on their way down. Thomas turned and started down a tunnel toward the entrance built over Cleopatra's Needle. "We're going to capture a hallow."

"How do we get it back here? Cab?"

"No," Thomas said, "but we will deal with that when the time comes. You will see, Squire, that there are other ways of movement than you have experienced."

"Stretch limo?"

Thomas snorted and said nothing further for the entire ride.

CHAPTER FOURTEEN

A GOOD CRY

Billie was about to follow Thomas into a cab just outside of Central Park when her partner suddenly stopped, half in, half out, then backed up to stand on the sidewalk, rudely shoving her to one side.

"Hold the cab," he said to her. Then he turned, as if listening to or talking on a cell phone, but there was no cell phone that Billie could see.

Billie stuck her head into the back door and said, "Hang on a moment."

The cabbie started to complain, telling her that he didn't have all night, so Billie just hit him with a simple comply spell. It was easy. Maybe too easy.

The driver nodded. He then got out of the cab, moved around to the front, leaned down on the hood, and began hugging the cab, making humping motions and moaning sounds.

Billie frantically searched her new knowledge, trying without luck to find an "undo comply" spell.

People started to stare as the cabbie got more and more passionate with the hood of his car, shouting in some strange language words Billie was glad she didn't understand.

Thomas had stepped off to one side of the sidewalk and was staring into the distance, as if he didn't notice the growing crowd.

"Undo!" she said, sort of twisting her arms into the air and aiming what she hoped was the right spell at the cabbie on the hood.

The cab fell apart, as if every bolt, every screw, every weld simply stopped holding. One tire rolled into the road and was hit by another cab.

The cabbie started taking off his clothes, all the while caressing his now useless pile of metal.

Thomas turned back to her. "Release the cab. We have a unicorn bleeding nearby."

She pointed to the pile of junk that had been their cab and the crowd gathering around to watch the cabdriver.

"You didn't try a spell, did you?"

Billie nodded. "Two, actually."

"No more, promise me," Thomas said. "Not until after you've had some more training."

"I promise," Billie said, trying not to look at the position the cabbie was getting himself into in relation to the grille.

Thomas shook his head. "I told Ethti having you on the street this quickly would be a bad idea after your first training session." He waved a hand. "Clear." Then he turned and walked off, expecting that she would just follow.

The cabbie seemed to wake up, then stared at his cab and started shouting.

"Thanks for waiting," she said softly to the cabbie. "We're not going to need you anymore." Then she ran after her partner, barely catching him just over a block away.

He started into a guarded building. She watched him as he put a don't-see spell on the doorman as they went inside.

They took an elevator to the seventh floor.

"Crime scene," one of New York's finest said, holding up his hand. "Just keep going."

Thomas flashed a badge while at the same moment passing his hand in front of the cop.

"Sorry, Detectives," the cop said, stepping back.

Billie made note of what Thomas had done.

Down the wide and thickly carpeted hall were two other uniformed policemen standing in front of an open apartment door. Thomas flashed them his badge and went inside to face two real detectives.

Billie stopped cold and stared at the unicorn lying on the wood entranceway floor. It was clearly dead, but there wasn't a drop of blood around it. And there was no sign at all of its human form.

"Clear the scene, please," Thomas said, holding up his badge and putting a comply spell on everyone in the room. A different comply spell than Billie had tried. Now she understood what she had done wrong with the cabbie. This magic stuff was going to take some serious practice.

"I'm Detective Hector Slice," Thomas said.

Billie managed to keep a straight face.

The two detectives started to move, but didn't seem happy about it. "You got something you want to tell us about the dead horse, Detective?"

"Dead horse?" Thomas said, staring at the man. "Have you been drinking, Detective?"

One of the men just outside the door snickered. The detective pointed at the body of what a moment ago had been a unicorn, but was now that of a middle-aged woman.

"Right there, the horse with the—" Both detectives stared at the woman.

Billie was just as surprised as the detective. Even she didn't see a Fantastic inside a human shell; this was just a human shell.

Thomas shook his head and waved a hand in front of all four cops, who were now staring openmouthed at the body, hitting them with what Billie knew was a cover-story spell. The same kind of spell he had tried to pull on her earlier. The one that hadn't worked.

"You have always seen a woman's body here. You will turn this case over to Detective Slice and be happy to be done with it."

Within thirty seconds the police were gone, pleased to move on and escape the paperwork. Even the man at the elevator left.

"Close the door," Thomas said, moving over and re-leasing the spell showing the old woman. Billie did as he instructed and then came back to watch him work over the unicorn. She had no idea what he was doing, but the death of the unicorn, for some reason, saddened her a great deal. She had been fed enough basic knowledge to understand that unicorns were loved by both Fantastics and humans, and were revered as the most magical of all creatures.

"Bled out," Thomas said, leaning back, clearly upset. "While she was still alive. Someone is using unicorn blood for a powerful spell."

"You're kidding?" Billie asked, shocked and feeling even more upset than she had a moment before.

"I am not," Thomas said, glancing up at her. "And contain your emotions. You are radiating."

Billie instantly understood what he meant. She didn't like it, but she understood. Her magical powers allowed her to radiate emotions to those around her. She had been given a simple magical spell to contain her emotions, but after the little problem with the cab, she was afraid to use it.

"Refresh me on that one," she said.

He quickly ran her through the three calming steps that formed the shield. The spell made her feel even worse, since all the emotions she had been sending outward now echoed back at her, as if she were contained in a tight ball.

"Good," Thomas said, nodding. "Release that spell only in your new, magic-guarded apartment after we are finished for the night. Understood?"

She glanced at the dead unicorn, then nodded. She knew that if her emotions were high enough, by projecting she could make everyone in a ten-block radius burst into tears.

It wouldn't do, of course, to inflict this kind of sadness on her unsuspecting neighbors, but as she looked at the exquisite lifeless creature, she couldn't help thinking that, whether they knew it or not, all of New York City needed a good cry.

CHAPTER FIFTEEN

PEEPING KNIGHT

Eve took the vials of unicorn blood carefully from the satchel that Snake Boy had carried them in. Carefully, making sure she didn't touch a drop of the blood, she poured the thick red liquid along each line of the complex diagram she had used to summon the power from Rallidae. She couldn't waste a drop, and couldn't miss reinforcing a line. Even with her new sense of strength and power, the job was slow and very tiring.

But worth it.

So far, the dark tan that symbolized her new power hadn't begun to fade. But she knew it would if she didn't get a second dose of Rallidae's energy twenty-four hours after the first, and then another hit the same number of hours later. She would need to repeat the ritual as many times as it took to make the powerful magic her own. It would mean killing a lot of unicorns and draining almost all the life out of Rallidae to attain the level she planned on reaching.

Then, and only then, would she be satisfied that no one could ever stand against her.

She finished her last line, touched up a few others with the last of the unicorn blood, then stood back. She was ready again, the diagram was ready again, and this time she knew it would work. All she had to do now was wait for the right moment.

"Return to the top of the staircase," she said, turning to Snake Boy. "Stand guard there until I send for you."

Snake Boy nodded like a bobble-headed dog in the back of a car.

"Challenge no one if they come through the door from the subway; simply come and wake me up. Understood?"

Again the nodding head.

"Now go," she said. "And no sleeping at your post."

On that command, he didn't nod as vigorously, and she had no doubt he would be asleep in an hour. She didn't care. She just didn't want him in the cave while she was sleeping. Her own magic shields were enough to wake her if someone tried to enter her cave.

She waited until Snake Boy's pounding steps faded up the stone staircase, then moved to a shielded private area of the cave, walking through what looked like a stone wall. On the other side was a luxurious room dominated by a huge satin-sheet-covered bed. A stone tub blended into the cliff face on one side, and a length of mirrors lined the other. Behind the mirrors were her closets, full of thousands of dresses.

She slipped out of her clothes, for a moment admiring her tan in the reflection. The dark skin seemed more beautiful than the pure white color. The ebony seemed to shimmer, hinting at rainbows of colors without ever showing them.

Power. Her color hinted at the power to come.

As she turned to admire her perfect body, a shimmering started in one side of one mirror. Then a face appeared.

Thomas.

She froze, shocked. How could he have found her and gotten through her screens? Or maybe he hadn't found her yet, just used a project spell to take his image to her.

His smile turned into a leer. "Having a little private mirror-mirror-on-the-wall time?"

She didn't even try to cover herself. Instead she stood there defiantly, staring back at the City Knight. He had seen her naked many times. Let him have another last look at what he had tossed out like so much trash.

"Long time, Tommy," she said, using a nickname that she knew he didn't like.

"Been to the beach?" he said. "Or are those tan lines from something else?"

"What I do with my life is my business these days," she said. "I no longer report to Ethti, or sleep in your bed. And how did you get into my mirror?"

"Security screens a little loose, huh?" He smiled. "Never was one of your strong suits."

She had him. The moment she asked, she knew it was only a project spell. He didn't really know where she was.

"You want strong?" she said, taking a deep breath and focusing her new power and strength into her security screens, into a spell to mislead Thomas as to her true location if he tried to trace her, and into a feedback loop aimed through his own project spell at him.

He shouted out in pain. The image shimmering in her mirror vanished.

"That will teach him to sneak into a woman's bedroom uninvited."

She laughed at the idea that he would have a headache for the rest of the night. Then, with one last look at her perfect body, she crawled into her warm, soft bed, letting the feel of the satin sheets against her skin soothe her.

Tomorrow, she would be even stronger.

The next night, stronger still.

Within a week, she would control the City Knights. Within two weeks, the entire world.

The thoughts made her smile. She drifted off into a perfectly restful sleep, counting her soon-to-be powers instead of sheep.

CHAPTER SIXTEEN

HOME, MAGIC, HOME

The night turned out to be the longest, and strangest, of Billie's entire life. She had started off as a night watchman at Bloomingdale's, chased a shoplifting troll, been force-fed magic lessons, kneeled at a crime scene over a murdered unicorn, and then captured an ancient hallow that stank.

Actually, she hadn't caught it; Thomas had. And "stank" didn't describe it. In fact, backed-up sewer smells would have been a pleasure compared to the smell coming from the naked, angry creature that they had captured running down the sidewalk outside of Bloomingdale's. Luckily, she hadn't been forced to actually touch the thing, but she had no doubt that her clothes were going to smell for a week.

Thomas had simply said, "Now watch and learn."

Then the hallow had vanished off the sidewalk.

She had no idea what Thomas had done; he hadn't made a single move.

"Did you learn anything?" he had asked.

"How would I know if I don't know what you did?"

He had just shaken his head and kept up the strong-and-silent routine, which was getting old fast. She did notice that every so often, when he did deign to speak to her, his New York way of acting and talking seemed to slip a little, as if he really wasn't from the city. Probably from Jersey.

After the hallow had been sent away to who-knew-where, they had spent the last few hours of the night making sure that no one saw the hallow, and that those who did had a cover story, including a reason why twenty store windows had been broken. She hadn't listened to so many lies in such a short period in her entire life.

By the time they had finished, the security alarms from the broken windows re-aroused her fading headache. She was tired, stunned, and just wanted to go to bed and wake up from this strange dream, or at least get a good shower to get the smell off. She needed to get to her old apartment and get her stuff, but Thomas had first wanted to take her to her new apartment, and saying no to him now seemed like it would take too much energy.

So she had agreed. Why not pile another thing into an already completely nutty night? What could it hurt?

In a new-looking black sedan, Thomas had driven her downtown to one of those many brick-and-stone buildings that you never noticed until you actually had to go inside for something. The thing looked fairly short compared with the structures towering above it. Maybe thirty stories at most.

He pulled into underground parking across the street and into an empty spot. "This is your reserved spot."

"I have a parking spot," she said, reverently. He had told her that earlier, and so had Ethti, but it hadn't sunk in. A private parking spot in Manhattan. Now, *this* was magic.

From the looks of things, the building had been a hotel at one time, then more than likely converted to apartments and sold off. He showed her past the doorman with a nod, then inside a narrow, very clean lobby area. She couldn't believe she was going to be living in a building with a doorman.

The elevator was old and wood-paneled, and looked slow. Thirty-four floors. But she could sense there was something magical about the elevator control panel. She couldn't see anything, or identify which spell was on the panel, but she could sense it, and after just one night with her new abilities, she was starting to trust that sense a little.

Not much. And not enough to try any spell again anytime soon.

Thomas started to reach for the panel and she stopped him. "Magic there," she said.

He smiled. "Very good, Squire. You are learning."

"So what's the deal?"

"Your floor is hidden."

"My floor?"

Thomas waved his hand over the panel, and the thirty-fifth-floor button appeared. "Go ahead. It's keyed to your touch only. Part of the security system."

She stared at the number, then glanced at Thomas. "I have the penthouse floor?"

"Of course you do," he said. "You're a squire training to be a City Knight."

"Other Knights don't live here?"

"We all have our own places on the tops of buildings around the area."

She still hadn't touched the button, leaving the two of them standing in an unmoving elevator on the ground floor. "So who had this apartment before me?"

"Benson," Thomas said, reaching over and touching the button for the floor below her floor. "But it was re-modeled and refurnished for you tonight."

The elevator jerked into motion, moving more quickly than she would have expected. "What happened to Benson?"

"Killed by a Ti-ti."

"In this apartment?" she asked, not exactly liking the idea of a murder scene in her new apartment.

Thomas laughed. "No, in South America, actually. A roving band of imps took over a tribe of Ti-ti, using them for their games. Benson went to help stop them and re-turn the Ti-ti to the jungle. He was killed when a Ti-ti hit him with a large branch and broke his neck."

Billie nodded, not having a clue what a Ti-ti was, and not really wanting to ask at this time of the morning, mostly out of fear Thomas might actually tell her.

"Are you going to push the button?" Thomas asked. "I'd like to go home and get a shower and get some sleep."

The elevator had just stopped on the top floor that non-magic people could see. She punched her floor's button before the elevator started back down.

The button disappeared the moment she took her fin-ger off. The elevator started upward, then stopped quickly and surely on her floor.

The door opened into the most fantastic view she could ever imagine an apartment having.

Ever.

Around the elevator was an entry area with a polished wood floor. Through a giant stone archway, long couches and chairs filled a thickly carpeted living room framed by massive windows ten feet tall. A roof garden beyond still had some late fall flowers in pots.

Sunrise painted the entire area in soft shades of orange and yellow. It was simply the brightest, most open space she could ever imagine existing in New York City.

"Wow," she said, softly, staring at the high ceilings, the soft-looking brown furniture, the original paintings on the walls. It was decorated exactly as she would have done, if she had about a half million to spend on furniture and paintings.

"Three rooms, two baths down the hall that way," Thomas said, pointing off to the left of the elevator core. He walked through the stone archway and pointed to the right. "Kitchen and dining against the windows there."

"Dining?" she asked, trying to get her mind to grasp what she was seeing. In her last apartment she didn't even have room for a small kitchen table.

Something had to be wrong. This couldn't be hers, yet the knowledge they had planted in her mind told her it was. Her starting salary for a squire was actually low compared with what she knew she would be making once she became a full Knight.

Yet this apartment, which was part of her salary, seemed just too much.

"Take your time, get used to the place," Thomas said, heading toward the elevator door. "I told the movers to put all your stuff from your old apartment in the second bedroom. You can sort it out when you get the time."

"All my stuff is here? Did I give notice at my old place?"

"Two weeks, but we moved you anyway," Thomas said, punching the elevator button. "Phone is on, food in the refrigerator and freezer. Get a shower and some sleep. You need to be in the Big Meeting Room at seven this evening, ready to work."

The elevator door slid open and he stepped in, turning to smile at her. "Good first night, Squire. Except for that cab thing. I'm glad you joined the team. Now release your emotion spell and get some sleep. I'll see you at seven."

With that the doors closed and Billie found herself alone, in the biggest, most wonderful penthouse apartment she could ever imagine.

She slowly walked through the place, touching everything, and then just standing and staring at her very own washer and dryer. They sat like alien creatures to one side of the second bathroom. She wasn't sure she would even know how to use them. There weren't any coin slots.

Finally, she found herself standing in the living area staring out the windows at the view looking uptown toward the park. She had no idea how she felt, besides tired and shocked. Everything was all bottled up.

It had all happened too fast.

Part of her mind kept insisting that this was all a dream. Or that someone was scamming her. People like her didn't have things like this happen to them. Adoptive parents, didn't finish high school, kicked out of the Marines. Yeah, she deserved this kind of place.

Right.

If she had any friends, she would be wondering who was playing the joke on her. Yet all that knowledge the City Knights had crammed into her brain told her that this was real. That her magic was real, that her double visions hadn't been caused by a head injury.

She had just hit the jackpot.

She took a deep breath and released the emotion-containment spell she had put on over the unicorn's body.

It felt like a dam broke inside of her.

—Mourning for the death of the beautiful creature.

—Excitement over getting the job.

—Fear at seeing this and maybe having it all taken away.

—Fear that she might not live up to Ethti's and Thomas's high expectations of her.

She let all the emotions come out, knowing that somehow the apartment kept them from going anywhere.

Then finally, drained, she just stood there, staring at the beautiful sunrise over the city she loved.

Her job now was to protect the city from creatures and forces of evil that twelve hours ago she couldn't even have imagined existed. Creatures that could destroy the city at any moment. The City Knights often gave their lives to protect the delicate balance between humans and Fantastics, and to protect one from the evil always lurking in the other.

Sure, they were giving her a nice apartment, a car, and a *parking space*, for heaven's sake. But deep in her heart she knew that after tonight, she would have done the job for free.

It was a noble job.

It made her feel the way she had felt being a marine, that there was a higher calling to her life.

A Knight's calling.

Chapter Seventeen

FIRST BLOOD

The next night her headache had faded back to a dull reminder and her ability to sense magic had increased. Now she could see faint auras around people and Fantastics who had magic. The brighter the colors, the stronger the magic, it seemed. Both Thomas and Ethti had very bright colors around them. Other City Knights had less vibrant auras. She didn't say anything to Thomas about this new ability, figuring he would just laugh at her. Or frown silently.

For the second night, the hallows flooded the city and every Knight from the entire surrounding area was called in to help, leaving Newark half defended from a rogue band of imps and Baltimore facing an infestation of mini-mites shorthanded.

She had given up asking where they were going as Thomas slid his car sideways across Forty-second Street, blocking the road. Ahead of them, car alarms were going off as if the world were about to end. Billie could see that three hallows had a poor woman and were playing catch with her.

"I'll get the two on the left," Thomas said as he jumped out of the car and started at a fast walk toward the hallows. "You take care of the one on the right, near the side-walk."

"How?" Billie asked. She had no idea what he wanted her to do exactly.

"Call this your first major on-the-job experience," Thomas said. "Try not to hurt anyone."

"Oh, great," she said. "At least the Marines trained their soldiers."

"This is basic training. It gets much worse than this."

The smell of the three hallows hit her before she could say anything more. A backed-up-public-toilet smell combined with the wet cardboard stink of a pulp mill. The air seemed so thick, she felt like she was wading upstream in sewage.

The hallows were still tossing the woman around as if they were passing a basketball. And the woman wasn't that small. These hallows were strong, and clearly didn't care about human life.

With a wave of his hand, Thomas knocked two hallows back and plucked the woman right out of the air. He put her down on the hood of a car as if he were placing a baby in a crib.

Billie was impressed. He looked so heroic and made the task seem simple.

"Stay here," he said to the woman. "You'll be fine. I'll be right back."

Her mouth gaped like a fish; then she nodded.

The hallow that Billie was supposed to be "taking care of" said something in Fantastic to her as she kept walking toward it. She was surprised that tonight she actually understood about half of what it said. None of it was nice. Something about humans and cattle. Or humans as cattle.

She could see that the hallow had a magic aura. Not a very bright one, but it was still there, so somehow her magic was going to have to help her beat this thing.

Maybe.

The hallow stepped toward her, a grin on its face showing ugly brown teeth. The smell was going to make her eyes water in a moment, and that wouldn't be good in a fight.

One thing the Marines had taught her about fighting was never pull a punch, and always land the first one.

Without breaking stride, she said, "You're coming with me."

The hallow started to say something back and she hit it squarely in the nose, trying to shove her fist through the thing's ugly head.

The punch landed solidly and the jarring rocked her, as well as the pain in her fist. Hopefully, she hadn't broken a knucklebone.

Her hand came away covered in brown ooze and smelling as if she had stuck it in a septic tank.

The hallow went over backward like a sack of flour, landing on the sidewalk with a sickening thud.

Billie took a deep breath and moved to the creature before it could get up. With a quick snap, she had both of the creature's slimy hands behind its back and her knee planted firmly between its shoulder blades.

She glanced around at where Thomas was facing both hallows, acting as if nothing was wrong. As Billie watched, they charged at him. The instant before they reached him, both hallows vanished.

Thomas then turned around, saw Billie, and shook his head.

She hated it when he shook his head like that.

"Now what did I do wrong?" she asked as he started toward her.

"Why didn't you use a spell?" Thomas asked.

After what she had done to that cabdriver and his poor sexually abused cab, she was afraid to try one. But she wasn't going to tell Thomas that.

"You hit Fantastics and all it does is make them angry," Thomas said, stopping beside the car with the woman sitting on the hood. "And when they get angry, they get really strong."

Then he turned to the woman. "You're going to be just fine."

Suddenly, under Billie, the hallow jerked, slipping free from her with incredible strength. The hallow shoved upward and she was sent flying back, a good ten feet off the ground. Thomas hadn't been kidding about the strength.

She somehow managed to come up with a magic spell that would cushion her landing a little as she smashed into the top of a parked van. It still hurt and knocked the wind out of her.

And it certainly didn't do the van any good. She had smashed the top and made a whole side panel collapse. Two nights on the job and she had managed to wreck two vehicles. She hoped they weren't going to take all the damage out of her paycheck.

She rolled off the van and landed in a fighting stance.

The hallow, clearly angry, was charging at her like a stinking bull.

Her Marine training told her to step sideways at the last moment and let the force of the opponent's forward motion help her toss it. But Thomas had been clear that she should use magic instead of her fists, so she used the first spell that came to mind.

She turned the sidewalk to a slippery slope.

Only one problem.

One very big problem.

She changed the *entire* sidewalk, all the way to Broadway.

The hallow lost its footing as she hoped it would and came sliding toward her.

But she lost her footing as well, along with a dozen people who were standing back watching, and another dozen people on the block toward Broadway.

As she fell, she could see Thomas just shaking his head. If he kept doing that, she was going to twist it right off his neck for him.

The hallow slid into her, getting its smell and brown gunk all over her. Before she could punch it again, it grabbed her by the foot and threw her toward a nearby brick wall.

She again put up a protect spell around her body as she hit, then dropped to the sidewalk like a bag of concrete. Even with the protect spell, that hurt like crazy. She was going to be sore for a week after this.

She tried to stand, but slipped and fell again before shutting off the slippery spell on the sidewalk.

The hallow came to its feet charging at her, clearly intending to do as much damage as it could.

She took a deep breath and dug down inside, into the knowledge that had been fed to her about her magic.

"Stop."

She held out her hand, palm forward, as she said the word.

The hallow stopped cold, but so did a dog that had been barking on the other side of the street behind the hallow. And so did the group of five people behind the dog who had been watching.

Frozen statues.

Again, Thomas just shook his head and stayed with the woman on the car.

Judging from the look of hatred in the frozen hallow's eyes, she was really pissing it off now. She released the spell. The hallow came at her, now really, really angry.

At the last moment, she imagined a net over the creature, a net impossible to break out of, holding it to the sidewalk.

A net appeared in the air and dropped over the hallow, forcing it to the ground.

Thomas clapped politely, the sounds of his clapping barely getting through the car alarms and police sirens echoing in the street between the buildings. Others in the crowd joined in the applause.

She didn't feel like bowing. She felt angry and banged up and really, really smelly.

Thomas excused himself from the woman and walked over to where Billie stood, covered in the smell and goo of the hallow. In all her life, she hadn't felt this stupid. She could have used the net spell before even punching the creature. Stupid, stupid, stupid.

"Very good," Thomas said.

"Yeah, right," she said, wanting to brush something off her forehead, but afraid to touch her face with her dirty hands.

"You didn't end up in the hospital," he said. "That's better than most squires after their first real-life training session."

"You're kidding?"

"Nope. But I was standing by to make sure you didn't get killed."

"Thanks," she said.

The hallow disappeared with a wave from Thomas. Later she would ask him where he was sending them, but right now she didn't much care. All she wanted was a hot shower and to burn these clothes.

But it took them another hour to clean up and spell all the people who had seen the fight, giving them cover stories that matched, yet didn't quite.

And then another hour after that having Thomas show her how to do a story spell that covered entire buildings and everyone in them, in case someone had been watching out the window and had gone back to bed.

By the time they were ready to leave, the stink from the hallow had caked on her skin like dried mud. Thomas wouldn't let her get into his car, so she ended up walking home. Not the best ending to her second night on the job.

CHAPTER EIGHTEEN

WHITE ROOM, TAKE TWO

Billie stared at the pure white room and the small red dot in the center. It had been one full week since the first time she had stood on that dot and had her mind filled with so much stuff that she was still trying to sort it out. Sometimes she didn't know what she didn't know.

The week had gone by so fast that she hadn't even had time to unpack most of her things. Luckily, her new apartment had come stocked, and the deli across the street was a good one. During the week, she and Thomas had captured almost two dozen of the naked, ancient sprites.

And every one seemed to smell a factor worse than the one before it, if that was possible. Now she was comparing the smell of the well-endowed small creatures to the smell of a human corpse buried on a garbage scow on the East River, *after* it had sat in the sun for a week.

Actually, she had to be honest with herself: Thomas had done all the heavy lifting. She had done some spells, like seeing through the security screen on her building's elevator panel, like implanting a new cover story in a confused man who had seen a hallow do a rude dance on the hood of his car. But none of that compared to what Thomas could do with one wave of his well-manicured hand.

After her first battle, she had always used the net to capture a hallow, and then let Thomas vanish them to wherever he was vanishing them to. Along the way, he had also trained her in dozens of spells, both small and large, but she still wasn't sure if she trusted herself to use them.

She had mentioned this fear to Thomas. He thought it was a good thing. "Always better to be afraid of your magic than too sure of it."

He said he would explain more later.

As the week had gone on, she had grown more and more comfortable with the idea of magic, with the idea that she had magic, with the idea that this world even existed. Now she didn't think she might wake up back in Iraq at any time. At least she had made that much progress.

Every night the hallows appeared. So far the worst damage, besides a lot of human injuries, was to the top of a few skyscrapers when a half dozen hallows had gotten into a playful fight using broken-off lightning rods and bricks as missiles between buildings. By the time a group of City Knights had stopped them, they had broken almost a hundred windows fifty stories in the air. A rampaging street gang had made a lame cover story on that one as far as Billie was concerned.

Over the week, no one could find the mysterious sorceress every hallow saw standing in the stream of energy coming from Rallidae, the ancient evil far below.

No ancient records mentioned anything about Rallidae. Just that the Last Great Unicorn King had trapped it there.

Billie had no doubt that it was going to get worse on the hallow level before it got better. And a lot worse on the big-evil and sorceress side of things. She could sense that, like knowing your time had run out on a meter and not being able to get back to it.

New York City was in danger.

"Are you going to just stand there all night?" Thomas asked.

Billie glanced back at him, then at Ethti, who was standing beside him. "When was the last time you used this room?"

"I never have," Thomas said. "We had different ways of training when I joined."

"Please," Ethti said, smiling at Billie. "The first time is the most disconcerting, I can promise you that."

Billie didn't want to ask her what the second time was known for. She stepped into the room and moved toward the red dot. Man, this place was white.

White, like a blinding snowstorm, only without the flakes and cold. White, like falling face-first into a pile of blank sheets of paper, only without the bump on the forehead, or the paper cuts.

Pure nothingness of white.

"About time," a voice said, booming around the room.

Billie knew that was the voice of the two-thousand-year-old wizard who taught the City Knights.

"Stand on the red dot."

She stopped on the red dot as the door thumped closed and then vanished into whiteness.

The next instant she was standing in a very color-filled room in front of Thomas. Only now Thomas looked more like a college professor than a cross between a professional football player and a model for *GQ*. He had on a Mets T-shirt and faded jeans.

There were many things she liked about Thomas. His hair was perfectly cut, and slightly long in the back. She liked that. And his smile could stop a train. She liked that, even though she hadn't seen him smile much this first week.

She didn't like him shaking his head at her.

This time Thomas wasn't shaking his head. Only smiling. Maybe she could talk him into coming back to her new apartment, talk about where they had met over a glass of wine, and maybe break in her new sheets.

Stop it. He's your partner.

She didn't want to ask him the obvious question, like where was she? So instead she forced herself to look away from him and glance at the room. Thousands of books filled dark oak shelves, some paperbacks, most older books in leather bindings. A fire crackled in a stone fireplace to her right, giving the room a faint smell of burning wood. A large oak desk covered with books and papers sat to her left, clearly often used.

Comfortable and lived-in was how the place felt.

And she had seen this place before.

"Sit down, Billie. We've got a lot to talk about."

Oh, hell. His deep blue eyes twinkled. They actually twinkled. Why hadn't she seen that before either?

"So where are we?" she managed to finally ask, pulling away from his gaze and turning her attention to the books. "Am I still in the white room in New York?"

"No, you're here," he said. "Here, as in a very deep cavern in England." He patted the desk affectionately. "My home country. Actually, the white room is only for show. You're powerful enough, you would have remembered this shortly."

"What, that I've been here before? Already feeling that."

He stared at her for a moment, then nodded. "I had a hunch you might be powerful enough to work through my cover spell given enough time. Your first week on the street has been impressive, for a squire."

"'Cause I didn't get killed?"

"Pretty much," he said.

He pulled on a shelf of books beside his desk and it swung open silently. Beyond the books was a room that looked a lot like an operating room, only without all the equipment. Just a single couch and chair beside it in the middle of the room. Nothing on the walls and everything painted the same dull color.

"This is where you got your knowledge last time."

Suddenly she remembered everything about her first visit to the white room, and her first visit to Thomas's office and learning area. It had taken an hour on the couch before Thomas had said she had had enough. She remembered thinking she could never get enough of staring into his blue eyes.

"So why hide all this?" she asked, glancing back at him. "I don't seem to remember it being that uncomfortable a learning process."

He laughed and sat down behind his desk, indicating that she should take a chair across from him as the door into the teaching room closed. "No one besides Ethti in the New York area of City Knights has actually met me in here."

"You mean no one actually remembers meeting you in here."

"Yes, that," he said, smiling.

"And I'm not going to either, right?"

He shrugged. "I doubt I could keep you from remembering this for very long, so I'm not going to try. I've never trained anyone who has the natural power you have. Not in over a thousand years of helping the City Knights train recruits."

"You know, I don't feel so powerful."

"Trust me, you are," Thomas said. "But you're still a squire, and it's going to take you years and years to control your full power. Maybe decades. All this session will do is take you another step along that road."

He stood and started to pace. She watched his perfectly proportioned body move like the body of a panther in a cage. "We have to thank the Fates that you arrived when you did."

"Excuse me?"

"Right now, in your city, the world is about to face a threat that could destroy everything. City Knights from all over the world are going to be coming to New York for the showdown, hoping to merge powers to defeat a force beyond any evil ever seen before."

Billie didn't much like the sound of *that* bad-movie trailer. She had been able to tell that during her first week things had gotten more and more tense around headquarters.

"So why is it good that I enlisted now?" she asked, almost afraid of the answer.

"Because," he said, "after we're through here today, you're going to be one of the most powerful sorceresses ever."

"Yeah, right. And bats will fly out of my ears."

"Well, I certainly hope not," Thomas said, laughing. "But the City Knights need your power and strength."

"Sure." She honestly didn't believe a word he was saying. She didn't feel powerful, didn't feel strong. She just felt confused and tired after a long week of chasing down stinking hallows. "Just give me a set of training wheels and I'm all set to go."

He laughed. "Don't worry, we won't expect you to know how to use your power, but we might ask you to lend some of your power to some of us, if the situation warrants."

"Lend?"

He nodded, very serious.

"I have no idea how I would do that."

"I know you don't, Squire," he said. "And I have to tell you, it might be dangerous to you as well. But we'll cross that bridge, as they say, when we get to it. Ready for more training?"

The hidden bookcase door swung open again, exposing the room and the couch.

"I suppose," she said. There was nothing else to say.

CHAPTER NINETEEN

A NEW BOSS IN TOWN

The training session had taken almost six hours. When they were finished, Thomas had nodded and helped Billie off the couch. "You are as powerful as I thought you would be."

This time she understood exactly what he was talking about. It scared her to death, but she understood. She had felt the same after finishing Marine basic training. She had learned skills others didn't have. Now it was up to her to use those new skills for the right reasons.

Billie glanced past Ethti at Thomas as he reported on the training session. For the first time, she could really see the outlines of his magic power flowing around him. Thomas had told her that there were very few people who could actually see the magic in a person. She was one of them. The magic around Ethti was orange and red, rich and thick. Same with Thomas.

With her new powers, she could also tell he was hiding something he didn't want to tell Ethti and her about. It appeared as a black void in his magic power lines, like a black rock in a stream of colored water. The secret concerned a woman named Eve.

Billie shook her head, hoping but not really expecting to rid herself of this little piece of inside information. She was pretty sure she didn't want to know something Thomas didn't want to tell her. Maybe a distraction would help. She interrupted a surprisingly heated exchange between Ethti and Thomas to ask about an upcoming meeting.

"The seers have seen a coming threat," Ethti snapped. During basic training, Billie had encountered a six-foot-three drill sergeant with a voice like a foghorn who wasn't as intimidating as this tiny woman.

"So they can see into the future?" Billie asked. "Then they already know how everything turns out."

"No, they only see places where different futures can branch," Ethti explained in a more patient tone. "A major branch is coming between continuing life and death to all humans."

"Now I'm sure I saw this in a movie trailer," Billie said.

Ethti glared. Thomas shook his damned head again. Billie wished she knew an anti-sweating spell. "The oldest, the most powerful City Knights from every part of the world will be coming here," Thomas said finally. "We can only hope it will be enough."

Deep in Billie's gut, down in the place where her new power and magic lived, in the place where what she used to think of as her "good instincts" dwelled, a nagging doubt grew. And that doubt formed a very clear thought in her mind.

It won't be enough.

Chapter Twenty

SPREADING THE SPRITES

In all her hundreds of years of being alive, Eve had never felt as good as she did now. She stared at the newly scored pattern on the floor, making sure that every line was again etched into the stone with fresh unicorn blood.

Every day she had stood in the pattern and soaked up the energy and power of Rallidae below. It had still not awoken, but she could tell she was disturbing it. By the time it did rouse from its century-long sleep, she would have its power and would be able to kill it easily.

Above her, the evening's release of hallows had caused the usual stir among the City Knights. Tonight she would cause even more problems. She now had the power to spread the energy, pushing hallows out over a wider area, causing even more damage.

"Increase my time in the flow by two minutes," she said to Snake Boy.

He looked worried, but said nothing.

She let her slinky white gown drop off her perfectly dark body.

Snake Boy gasped, just as she had when she first saw her perfect body and shining ebony skin in the mirror after the second day.

Her hair had turned pure black and had grown longer by almost a foot. Her skin was so shiny now that she could see reflections in it when she took a bath. The pupils of her eyes had also turned dark, as had her magic aura flowing around her.

Luckily, she loved darkness.

She turned slowly, giving Snake Boy an eyeful of her nakedness. "Like what you see?"

"Of course," he said, a little too quickly, with a little too much head-nodding.

"Start the camera," she said, stepping carefully into the middle of the pattern, making sure not to touch any unicorn blood.

"Camera started," Snake Boy said.

"Start the timer," she said.

"Timer started."

"Awake!" she shouted, thrusting both hands toward the roof of the cavern. "Awake!"

Twelve seconds later a burst of dark energy poured up through the pattern and over her body. She let the feeling of a thousand spiders crawling over her skin take her into pure bliss as she soaked up the energy of the oldest evil known to the world.

Naked hallows flashed past her.

She willed them outward and upward, breaking the stream of energy after it had gone past her. No point in making it too simple for the idiot City Knights.

Over two hundred hallows had passed her by the time Snake Boy shouted "Time!"

She shut down the energy flow, stepped out of the pattern, and slumped to the hard rock floor. Every nerve in her body was vibrating with the new power she had taken in. Two minutes more than she had taken at any time before.

She let her senses roam out over the city, checking on what she had done. She had managed to spread the hallows over a circle thirty blocks in diameter, and as expected, they were causing their normal problems.

And a few new ones as well.

She laughed as she stood, letting Snake Boy help her into her robe. "I'd like to sleep now. Then later tonight, we'll find another unicorn. Go to the top of the stairs and guard me with your life."

Snake Boy nodded and left.

She was halfway to her bed when she felt something she had never felt before. Her new powers were working, and she could sense all the power in the city. She let the new learning in, absorbed it, studied it.

Someone as powerful as she was at the moment was in the city.

Two of them, actually.

She could feel their distinct magic patterns. Both of them were more powerful than Ethti.

Eve made no attempt to discover who they were. That could wait until later. She checked all her defenses and screens, using her newly gained power to bolster everything, including her hiding spell. There would be enough time later to deal with the others. She had only a few more days until the final night, the most important night of all.

All Hallows' Eve. The night before All Saints' Day. The most magically charged night of the year. On that night she would release all the remaining sprites into the world, take the last energy and power from the great evil, and then move to control the world.

It would be a night she would always remember.

A night the world would remember—at least, those who were left alive after it was over.

CHAPTER TWENTY-ONE

STINKY ISLAND

They were two blocks up from the United Nations building. Thomas took on a band of hallows, leaving Billie to face down two at once. Another first for her.

"Hey, stink machines," she said in Fantastic, pointing at the two hallows who were taking turns shoving cars through store windows. "Cut that out."

"A human who speaks," one hallow said.

"I am disgusted," the other said.

Billie winced at the grating squeal of their voices. Sometimes she was sorry that the second training session had refined her ability to understand and speak all the different levels of Fantastic.

"We shall teach the beast a lesson of respect," one said as both hallows started to come at her.

She covered one with a net, letting it scream and swear at her.

"Sorry. School's out," Billie said as she turned her attention to the other hallow.

It somehow blocked her net and got away, climbing up the side of a building faster than a rat scampering toward a pile of garbage.

She had to follow it.

She dug down into her new knowledge and came up with a gravity-shifting spell. Making sure that it applied only to her and not to everything on the street around her, she tipped gravity ninety degrees and ran up the wall after the hallow.

For the first ten floors, it was really cool. The biggest problem was jumping over the floor ledges.

About twenty floors up she started to question herself.

At thirty floors, her vision suddenly took over and she realized exactly what she was doing.

Her mind screamed, *This isn't possible!*

The small, calm part kept repeating, *Trust your magic. Trust your magic.*

Screw the magic. This isn't possible!

A moment later she found herself falling back toward the street, the spell gone. Not even an impact-buffering spell was going to stop this from hurting a great deal. Or worse.

"Thomas!" she shouted.

He didn't hear her. Or, worse, he ignored her as he tried to contain a group of the hallows.

She frantically searched for anything that might help. Finally, she decided to turn the sidewalk to deep, soft rubber. She also wrapped an impact spell around herself.

It worked.

Except for one problem.

She bounced as if she had hit a trampoline.

"Would you stop fooling around with your magic and get that hallow!" Thomas ordered as she hit the top of a parked car ten feet from him and smashed out every window.

Another vehicle destroyed. Great. She was a one-woman demolition derby.

"He's gone up the building," she said, rolling off the car and facing Thomas, who had his hands full with six hallows blocking his transport spell.

"So go get him," Thomas said as he tricked two hallows away from the others and sent them off to who-knew-where.

"I'm not Spider-Man," she said.

"Use gravity to your advantage," he said.

She was starting to point to the smashed car, to tell him that was exactly what she had tried to do, when she got another idea.

She moved back and looked up. The hallow was using a piss-poor invisibility spell to hide on a ledge forty or so floors up. Using her best aim, she changed gravity around the hallow, making him far, far heavier than he had been a moment before.

The action tipped him off the ledge and he fell toward the street.

Once he was in midair, she released her spell and just let him drop.

He smashed into the roof of another parked car, destroying it.

She dropped a net over the creature as it lay there, stunned.

"You come up with the cover story for those," Thomas said, finishing up with the gang of hallows.

"Give me a minute," she said.

He shook his head again and then moved over to the first hallow she had captured and sent it off.

"Where are you sending them to?"

"I'll show you," Thomas said. "Your net secure?"

"Secure as I can make it," Billie said, glancing at the hallow trapped in the net on top of the ruined car.

"Then hang on to it," he said.

"Hang on to it?"

"With your mind, wrap the ends together as if you are carrying the hallow in a sack."

She did as he told her to do.

"Got it," she said. "I think."

With that, Billie found herself and her containment net with the hallow on a wide, sandy beach. The sun was high in the sky and hot, the air smelled of the ocean, the wind was fresh and off the gentle waves.

The hallow screamed and covered its eyes, cowering on the sand.

"Let it go," Thomas said.

Billie dissolved the net and the hallow ran for the shade of the jungle just off the beach, making "ouch"-like noises as it tried to keep its bare feet off the hot sand and run at the same time.

It disappeared into the jungle with a crashing of brush. Over the jungle, she could see a couple of pretty decent-sized mountains.

"We're dumping them here," Thomas said.

"No humans?"

"Not a one. We call the place Unnamed Island. It lies a thousand miles east of New Zealand."

"Food is natural, huh?" Billie said.

"More than enough to eat, more than enough room to move around, no humans, and no way for the hallows to leave."

"Isn't there a television show about a plane crashing on an island like this?"

Thomas looked at her like she was crazy. "Could never happen."

"Fine," she said.

The sun was hot on her white skin. She looked around, almost afraid to move for fear of getting too much of the light sand in her shoes.

The perfect prison. She could see the magic field covering the island a few hundred feet off the shore. A visual shield and physical shield in one. Very strong and powerful.

And very old.

"No one gets in or out, huh?"

"Exactly," Thomas said. "Not even a passing ship can see the island."

"How long have you guys been using this island for this kind of thing?"

"Since before I was born," Thomas said.

"That long, huh?" Billie said, and smiled at him.

She did one more scan of the island. "So we don't kill or torture the hallows, just let them spend the rest of their lives playing tricks on each other in a tropical paradise. Who else is here?"

"Trolls, a bunch of nymphs, about fifty gnomes, and a dozen other creatures."

"A tropical-paradise prison for the Fantastic criminals we can't fix easily."

"Exactly," Thomas said, laughing, his blue eyes twinkling even more in the bright light. "But one thing. Always remember when you are coming here to land on a beach upwind from the main jungle and mountains of the island. There are already hundreds of ancient hallows on this island. The smell is growing by the day."

She laughed. "Got it. Now let's go find more."

"Good idea," he said. "You want to take us back?"

She stared into those wonderful eyes of his for a moment, trying to see if he was serious. He clearly was.

"Check in with your magic," he said. "Just like every training session we have done, always remember to check in with your magic. It's where your power is."

She nodded. "So I can do the appearing and disappearing and jumping-from-one-place-to-another thing?"

"You tell me," he said. He wiped a bead of sweat off his forehead. "Just don't take too long. I don't want to get sunburned out here."

She nodded and went deep inside herself, using the imaginary staircase that he had taught her to visualize in their last session yesterday. He had trained her to reach the bottom of the staircase. There she had stored all her magic spells and powers. She simply found the power she needed to use. Then used it. After that, to use that power, she would not need to use the staircase image again. It would be under her instant control.

Down, down she went, ignoring the heat of the island around her, until she finally stepped off the bottom step onto what she called her power platform. She felt invincible on the platform, something he had taught her to feel.

She liked that feeling, maybe a little too much.

Using her new ability to see things from great distances, she searched for where they had been in New York, just down from the UN building. She could see the street as clearly as if she were standing there.

Almost like Dorothy in the *Wizard of Oz* movie, she visualized being there. She didn't click her tennis-shoe heels together, but for an instant she thought about it.

The sound of waves, the heat of the sun, were replaced by the noise of traffic and the cold of the night air in the city. Familiar noise.

Familiar cold.

She started to say something to Thomas, then glanced around and shook her head. "Damn, forgot him."

An instant later he was beside her, laughing. "Last time I take you to the beach, Squire."

Billie laughed as well. She could feel that her face was turning red, and not from the sun.

"I think we'd better get back to work," Thomas said. "We have a long night ahead of us." Thomas smiled at her, his blue eyes again twinkling in the streetlights.

"Next sighting?" she asked.

"Two blocks over," Thomas said.

Thomas flashed them there in an instant, and this time she took the captured hallow to the island by herself, letting Thomas know where she was going, of course.

She might be able to do something with all this magic, but she still didn't trust herself to get it right every time.

CHAPTER TWENTY-TWO

ALL ABOUT EVE

The sun was coming up as Thomas led Billie into a deli across from the Crowne Plaza Hotel on Broadway. Between the two of them, they had captured over thirty hallows. A very good night's work.

A *long* night's work.

And Billie had had only the one incident, and destroyed only two cars. She was improving very quickly. He would have to be careful to remember that she was still very new at all this and keep an eye on her.

The deli had a wonderful breakfast smell of frying bacon and freshly baked bread. The glass case in front of him was filled with wonderful-looking pies and cakes, but he ignored them and ordered off the menu board over the grill. Two eggs, hash browns, bacon, and toast, along with a glass of orange juice. Then, after getting his food, he went up a narrow flight of stairs to a small dining area in the back.

Two men in dark suits and narrow ties sat upstairs, near the back, reading the morning paper. He ignored them and they ignored him, even though he knew who they were and was sure they knew who he was as well. Not saying anything was just better for both sides.

He sat down at a table overlooking the deli below and didn't wait for Billie to join him before eating. He hadn't realized just how hungry he had gotten.

"How are you feeling?" he asked between wonderful bites of eggs as she joined him at the table.

"Like I need a good eight hours' sleep."

He watched, shaking his head as she poured ketchup over her scrambled eggs and then salted them heavily.

The two ate in silence for a moment. After her first few bites, Billie asked without looking up at him, "You want to tell me about Eve?"

The bite of toast went dry in his mouth. He stared at her until she looked up, clearly embarrassed that she had even asked the question.

"You want to repeat that?"

"Something about a woman named Eve is bothering you," Billie said. "And it seemed to be getting worse as the night went on. Or maybe I just noticed it more than before."

"How do you know about her?" he asked, not really wanting to believe she had asked about Eve. She was just a squire and his business was his business.

Billie pointed to a place right beside his head, poking her finger at something that he couldn't see. "There's a black place in your magic aura, and when I focus on it, the name Eve comes to mind."

"You can see that much in my magic?" He was surprised. It was another sign of just how powerful she was going to be in a few years. If she survived.

She nodded.

His first inclination was to tell her to mind her own business and never use her magic to pry in that way again. But he had been worried that Eve was behind the hallows and the problems that were coming. And he had planned on talking to Ethti about it every day, but had kept hesitating. He didn't know how Eve *could* be responsible.

He knew that he hated her beyond any reason. On their last meeting, she had actually laughed at him. Except for the way she shut down his mirror search for her, he had no evidence that she had gained power since the last time they were together. So, as each day had gone by, he couldn't decide if this was business or personal. Very personal.

"Don't want to talk about her?" Billie said, staring into her plate. "Fine. Sorry I asked."

"My ex-wife," Thomas said, letting out a breath he didn't know he'd been holding. "Elspeth."

"Ex-wife?" Billie sat back, clearly stunned. She was only twenty-one. She had no idea how much living could be done in centuries of time. He actually had five ex-wives, but he wasn't going to tell her that at the moment.

"We were married for a few years, a long time ago. She has gone by Eve for the last hundred years or so."

"When was the last time you saw her?"

"I haven't actually seen her face-to-face in at least a decade, although I tried to talk to her six days ago through her mirror, without any real luck. She cut me off, and cut me off *hard*. We, uh, don't get along."

It felt good telling someone all this, even if it was just his squire.

"You think she might be the sorceress the hallows see in the energy stream?"

"I don't know, actually," Thomas said. "She loved to study the old myths, dig into the old texts, find spells that had been lost for centuries." He shrugged and pushed his plate away. "She might have come up with something."

"But that's not why you think she might be the one, is it?" Billie asked.

Thomas shook his head. "She was never very powerful, so she was always incredibly power-hungry. She could just never accept herself and her level of magic. When Ethti came in and took charge of this area of City Knights, Eve left."

"Eve thought she should run the place?"

"She did. She considered herself more powerful than Ethti, and a better leader. It drove her crazy when she didn't get the job. Actually, she was never considered for the job."

"And she holds a grudge?" Billie asked.

Thomas couldn't stop the laugh. "Of course. She is the most bitter and self-centered person I have ever known. Not sure why I married her, to be honest with you."

Billie again patted Thomas's arm. "As you said, it was a long time ago."

"Not long enough, it seems."

"You said you tried to contact her. Does that mean you know where she is?"

The frustration he had been feeling pulled at him like a current in a river. "I've been trying to figure out where she is for seven days, since we learned that the hallows were seeing a sorceress in the energy stream. Nothing. Not a clue. I talked to her through her mirror for only a moment, but she had her location blocked. And she gave me one amazing headache when she cut me off. I've been thinking of trying a trace spell ever since, but just haven't had the time."

"Trace spell," Billie asked.

"It usually helps find lost spouses and children."

"Well, looks like we got some time now."

Thomas wanted to argue, but he knew the kid was right. Reluctantly, he closed his eyes and focused on the woman he had once loved, the woman he now hated totally and completely.

For the next ten minutes, as his breakfast got cold and the grease on the hash browns congealed, he searched the world for Eve.

No luck.

Nothing.

Not even a sense of her.

Eve had vanished from the planet. That scared the hell out of him. More than he wanted to admit. She hadn't been that powerful before, but she clearly was now.

Finally, he opened his eyes. "She's the one. I know it. Before, she didn't have the power to hide like that. I always knew where she was, even when I wasn't looking for her."

Billie only nodded, saying nothing.

"She must be the one gaining magic from the energy stream. Black magic. I have a hunch she's not doing this because of the hallows, but to gain the magic for herself."

Again Billie only nodded, staring at her almost empty plate of food.

The idea of his ex-wife's sudden power surge scared him. She had no common sense, and didn't care about anything that didn't benefit her in some fashion.

"We can't let her keep collecting power," he said. "She's already got a lot of it if she can hide from me. Now the question is, can we stop her? I've got to talk to Ethti and the council."

Billie said nothing and didn't look at him or anything else but her plate. He was so wrapped up in his own thoughts that he didn't notice that something was wrong with his squire. Very wrong.

Chapter Twenty-three

HIDING IN PLAIN SIGHT

Eve lay on the satin sheets that covered her bed, her beautiful dark sorceress body nude and shining under her reading light. Her eyes were closed, her hands crossed over her chest in a position of power.

She wasn't there, though.

Her mind floated above the street hundreds of feet overhead, watching the sun come up, watching the city come alive with all the magicless ants who scurried about doing their daily chores. They were almost beneath her notice now.

She watched for a moment as a dragon disguised as a human baker worked his ovens, getting ready for the coming rush.

At one point she had felt a slight tingling, a warning that someone was looking for her with magic.

Thomas.

Again.

Thomas, the idiot from the caves of England. One of the bigger mistakes of her life. Why had she ever bothered to marry him? She had been so stupid, so young, so weak.

She laughed at his pathetic attempts to find her, to track her, to bring her to him. He tried it all, but she stayed hidden. To think that at one point she considered him powerful. What a joke.

At one point, she thought about revealing herself to him, then decided it was better to continue to follow her plan. So instead she just drifted along with his search, never showing herself, laughing at the entertainment of it all, until finally he gave up and returned to his poor, ugly body sitting in a deli on Broadway.

A young woman sat with him, a young squire that she didn't know.

Eve let her mind drift in and around the table, listening to Thomas discuss her. He had finally figured out that she was the one letting the hallows loose on the city, and he knew what she was doing with the energy stream. He just didn't know where she was.

Or how to stop her.

She laughed at the idea that he or anyone else thought they *could* stop her.

She laughed at how slow he had been to figure out that she was doing what she was doing.

For a few moments, she studied the raw, young magic of the new woman. Interesting, not like any new magic she had seen before. She would have to pay attention to the young sorceress when the final time came. But the girl was so untrained, she couldn't even sense Eve's intrusion on their little breakfast. Too bad that the girl would never have the years and decades it would take to really learn her powers.

Eve then let herself return to her own body, her own bed, enjoying the feel of the satin sheets as she stretched. She needed the rest. Just two more nights until All Hallows' Eve, two more long drinks of power, and everyone would face her beauty.

And her anger.

The first to go would be the City Knights. All except Thomas. Him she would keep in a pen, just the way he tried to imprison her in so many ways when they were married.

He would be worth the entertainment value, if nothing else.

CHAPTER TWENTY-FOUR

NO HELP FROM OUR FRIENDS

As Eve vanished, Billie instantly tried to put up a shield spell.

As Thomas had trained her to do, she checked it to make sure that no one could get through magically without her knowing it.

It wasn't solid enough.

No way it could block Eve if she came back.

As an ex-marine, Billie could deal with someone coming at her with a physical weapon. But magical self-defense . . . Well, so far even her best efforts didn't seem to be doing her much good.

"At least she's gone for now. That's something," she finally said, letting the shivers that she had been containing get out to do a quick run up and then back down her spine. It had been so difficult to not say anything to Thomas while the disgusting power of Eve crawled around their table, watching them.

"Who's gone?" Thomas asked.

Thomas looked puzzled, and Billie suddenly realized that he didn't know that Eve had been there.

"Eve, I think. She was watching us."

Instantly she could feel Thomas's shield spell meld with hers, as if they belonged together. She could see the bubble around her grow more stable, more rocklike by a factor of thousands. It made her feel stronger, better, more confident. Maybe, at some point, they could do more melding spells. She pushed that thought away for the moment and faced him.

"Your shield was a good try for the first time," Thomas said, nodding to her with a look of approval in his eyes. "And the right thing to do after she left."

Billie smiled. She wasn't sure if she believed him, but it was nice of him to say something positive anyway.

Thomas leaned in closer to Billie. "So she protected herself from me, but she didn't know you would be here as well. And with enough untrained magic to see her."

"I suppose." Billie shrugged. "She studied me, though. Didn't let her know that I could see her, though, so she paid no attention to me, other than a last, quick look before she left."

"Very smart," Thomas said, smiling at her with that wonderful smile of his. "She has become *very* powerful if she could block my awareness of her. And if she is taking in the energy of the ancient creature trapped below us, it will control her, turn her into a dark sorceress."

Billie had no idea just exactly what a dark sorceress was, but it didn't sound good, and after her brush with Eve, it didn't feel good either.

"Luckily, she underestimated you."

"Yeah, luckily." Billie didn't feel lucky. She just felt dirty, far dirtier than she did after wrestling with a hallow.

"Think you can follow her home?" Thomas asked, staring at Billie.

"How?"

"Just sense her magic," Thomas said, putting his hand gently on hers. "Then let your magic go to her. I'll help you."

"Okay," Billie said warily, wanting—no, needing—to trust him. "Just go slow and take me step by step and I'll try."

"I'll do that. Now, close your eyes and focus on Eve and how she floated around us here."

She closed her eyes, letting the sounds of the deli and the smells of the food drift away.

Thomas was no longer speaking out loud, but she could tell he was beside her.

Carefully, she eased her way through the magic shield, as if she were sticking her head above water in a clear pool.

Eve's dark presence still hovered around them, like a foul-smelling cloud of cigarette smoke.

I see it.

Good. Thomas's thought came back as if it were one of her own. *Follow it the way you would follow an animal's tracks.*

And how would I do that?

Trust me to keep your mind afloat. Imagine just following what you see.

The next instant, Billie found herself hovering over the block not far from Bloomingdale's. She knew her body still sat in the deli on Broadway, could still feel the chair under her butt, but her mind, with a phantom body that looked and felt just like her real one, floated in the air.

Weird feeling. Real weird.

Squire. Don't think about what you are doing. Just do it and trust me.

Understood.

She focused on the foul trail of Eve, then went down.

Through the buildings, which seemed just wrong.

Very wrong. One man in an apartment was taking a shower as she passed. She saw far more in a glimpse than she ever wanted to see.

This can't be happening.

Trust me. Just follow the trail.

Down through the subway, through rock, through a nest of rats that made her shudder and almost stop.

Finally, she reached a cavern, heavily protected by magic spells. Black, swirling bubbles, like oil covering water.

She instantly willed herself back to the deli and opened her eyes to make sure she was back and grounded. The smells of the wonderful food anchored her and she kept her eyes wide open, letting the dizzy feeling pass.

Again, she had a headache. A bad one.

And she was more exhausted than she could remember ever being.

"We need to tell Ethti and a few others about what we have found," Thomas said.

"I suppose a nap first is out of the question?" she asked, knowing the answer.

"Not yet. I need you with me, Squire. You have done well."

She didn't have the energy to thank him, so instead she just nodded and pushed herself to her feet, moving carefully to make sure her breakfast stayed where it belonged. Going from floating through walls to walking seemed very odd.

Slowly, with Thomas staying at her side to keep her stable, they headed for the staircase down to the main level of the deli.

One of the men in black suits who had been reading a newspaper near the staircase glanced up at Thomas as they passed. "Good luck. Let us know if we can help."

"Thanks," Thomas said. "I will."

"Who was that?" Billie asked, glancing back as she and Thomas made their way toward the front door.

"Just friends of the City Knights," Thomas said. "But they can't help us. This problem is way out of their area."

CHAPTER TWENTY-FIVE

BIG BIRD TO BIG SLUG

Ethti's office felt hot. Billie wasn't sure if the heat was caused by the extra shields Ethti had put up or just by the fact that the air system was shut off. Either way, after five minutes Billie was sweating and Thomas had shed his thick sweater, leaving only a T-shirt on. He looked really, *really* good in a T-shirt.

Ethti paced as Billie told her what she had seen in the restaurant, then told her about helping Thomas follow Eve to the cave under the city, all the while trying not to stare at Thomas and his perfect, sweating body.

"So we know who is doing this now," Ethti said, nodding. "Good work, you two."

"And we know where she hides," Thomas said. "Now we need to discover exactly what this Rallidae creature is that she is getting the power from."

"We may be able to find that out as well," Ethti said.

Billie didn't even want to breathe as the room became deathly silent, and she waited for Ethti to go on. Billie wasn't sure she wanted to know exactly what could be this powerful. It might mean that they would have to fight it. And at the moment she was so tired that she doubted she could fight a full battle with a butterfly and win.

Around them, the windows to the main area of the huge office cave suddenly went opaque.

Ethti moved to the back of her office as a door appeared in the rock wall and slid open. Another hidden room? Billie supposed she shouldn't be surprised, but she was anyway. She thought she knew every detail of the City Knights headquarters, right down to where one hundred and twenty-seven bathrooms were.

Ethti indicated that everyone should follow her.

"What's back here?" Billie whispered to Thomas.

"Resource library," Thomas said, not even attempting to keep his voice down. "Some of the oldest documents in all the Earth reside here. Only City Knights have access to it, and then only with permission."

"Oh," Billie said, as she walked through the door and into a library that equaled in size anything she had ever seen. "Should I be in here?"

"Squires get tours of this place," Ethti said, her voice abrupt and dismissive. "Consider this one of your tours."

Billie nodded and just stared. The cave would swallow the main branch of the New York Public Library, building, lions, and all. It seemed to go on into the distance in three directions. It was far bigger than the huge area where the paper pushers worked.

Compared with the heat and bright light of Ethti's office, the cave seemed dark, cold, and very dry. Billie could almost feel her lips chapping as she walked down the main aisle.

A faint odor of old paper filled the air, but not a whiff of mold in any form. She could see that the cave was also well protected with magic. A very old, very powerful shield covered it.

"Amazing, isn't it?" Thomas said. "I have been in here a thousand times and I still feel the weight of history this room contains. A copy of everything every written about magic and the Fantastics is right here."

Unable to reply coherently, Billie barely managed a silent nod. She was just too stunned to talk. Tired and stunned. Not a good combination for clear thinking.

Ethti moved to a circle on the floor at an intersection between long, wide aisles, stepped into it, and muttered a few words.

Images seemed to swirl around her in the air as she stood there calmly studying them. They were moving faster than Billie could follow.

"Now what is she doing?" Billie asked Thomas.

"Looking up what she's searching for," Thomas said. "This room has a system that records every document here, as well as when anyone touches any document."

Suddenly Billie realized just why Ethti was searching the records. "She's trying to find the documents Eve studied when she was still here. Right?"

Thomas nodded. "She loved this place and spent years in here doing research on old spells."

"Stop!" Ethti said. She studied something for a moment hanging in front of her, then nodded and stepped through the floating card catalogue, causing the images to vanish. She headed down a side aisle between eight-foot-tall shelves covered with what looked like very old scrolls of some type.

Thomas followed close behind her. Billie brought up the rear, trying to take in every detail she could as they walked. At least three city blocks of a hike later, Ethti stopped, pulled out one scroll, said a quick magic spell of protection for the old document, then opened it, holding it up carefully for Thomas to see.

"This was a document that Eve spent a lot of time studying right before she left us."

"Rallidae?" Thomas asked, reading the top of the scroll. "Does it say what it was?"

Billie could see that the writing was in an ancient form of Fantastic. She could make out some words, but not all.

"Rallidae, an ancient bird god," Ethti said. "A scavenger, rumored to have turned evil before recorded history. It was said that he controlled a large part of the world for centuries."

"Oh, great," Billie said.

Ethti kept reading. "It seems that Rallidae's main priest was a crake named Porzana. Porzana was power-hungry and pushed Rallidae to take over the entire world by taking the power of other Fantastics."

"I suspect that didn't go over well," Thomas said.

"It caused a great war," Ethti said, studying the document. "Porzana was killed by a rampaging army of elves who shot the bird priest from the air with magic arrows."

"Nice aim," Billie said.

"In a great final battle, the Last Great Unicorn King changed Rallidae into a giant slug, one of Rallidae's favorite foods, and trapped the slug in an ancient hallows far under a distant island. There, he was to sleep for all time, guarded by the evil hallows who sided with him. All magic was stripped from all birds from that day forward."

"Birds used to have magic?" Billie asked.

Ethti ignored her question and looked at Thomas. "It says that unicorns gave their blood so that Rallidae could be transformed and imprisoned indefinitely."

"That explains a lot," Thomas said to himself. "Unicorns are dying now. Being bled. And Eve is using the blood to break the old spell, penetrate the hallows, and free Rallidae."

Silence filled the great library.

Ethti nodded.

Billie didn't want the image of the dead unicorn she had seen back in her mind, but now it was there. Only true evil could harm such a pure and gentle creature. It seemed that was exactly what they were facing. A very old evil.

"Eve is not yet finished," Ethti said, staring at the scroll. "To finally release the spell of the ancient prison, this document says it would take the power of All Hallows' Eve."

"That's tomorrow night," Thomas said.

Billie could feel her stomach twisting at how close they were to the end of the world. It felt the same as the night before a big firefight in Iraq.

"So we protect the unicorns," Thomas said. "All of them. Stop her that way."

"She needs help in the bleeding," Ethti said. "If I remember my old spells correctly."

"That's right," Thomas said. "He who stands in the power circle cannot be the one to do the bleeding."

If you say so, Billie thought, but was wise enough not to say aloud.

"A mortal is helping her," Thomas said. "It has to be. We protect the unicorns, find the mortal, and we will stop her."

"Possibly," Ethti said, still staring at the scroll. "But we may be too late to stop the awakening of Rallidae. If she is using an ancient draining spell, she has broken through the entrapment that has kept Rallidae in the hallows. If he wakes, the entrapment spell will no longer contain him."

"Why would she release an evil greater than her own powers?" Thomas said. "That's not like Eve. She would want to control everything, not serve an ancient bird god."

"She thinks she is draining its powers," Ethti said, her voice soft and shaking.

Billie never expected to see Ethti shaken like this, and it scared her. In the Marines, you never wanted to see your leaders worried.

Ethti carefully put the scroll back where it belonged, took a deep breath, and turned to face Thomas, ignoring Billie completely.

"No matter how much she has augmented her powers, it's clear Eve's judgment hasn't improved. Her plan will backfire. She can't harness Rallidae's power; she'll only anger it more. And if it escapes from the entrapment of the hallows that surround it, no force left on this earth will be able to stand in its way. We are doomed if we don't stop her."

"So," Thomas said, "at least we have a plan, now. We stop Eve, then seal the damage on the entrapment around the hallows before Rallidae wakes up. Seems straightforward enough."

Ethti said nothing.

Billie stared at her mentor, remembering the feel of Eve hovering around them at the table, the power of her shields, the dark evil of her magic. Thomas had a straightforward plan, maybe. But Billie had a hunch that carrying it out was much easier said than done.

Chapter Twenty-six

STOPPING THE BLEEDING

En route to the Big Meeting Room, Thomas told Billie that the meeting would be relayed to all ten major regional headquarters of the City Knights in the U.S., along with both the Canadian and Mexican branches. The council was standing by too.

Now Billie was really impressed, and even more frightened. In their sessions, Thomas had given her the entire history and management structure of the City Knights. New York, with Ethti in charge, controlled the thirteen North American branches of the Knights. Around the world, there were another sixty-seven branches, with the vast majority of those in Britain and Europe.

Over all the branches was the council, a group of nine powerful wizards and sorceresses, supposedly descendants of the great ones who brokered the treaty between humans and Fantastics. Thomas had told her that he couldn't even remember when the last time was that the council had met. Seems that had now changed.

It figured that the first person she spotted when she arrived in the room was good old Austin, sitting in the third row back, glaring at her. Someday he was going to have to get past the shield-cracking incident.

Billie smiled at him. He was pathetic and weak. Billie could see his spotted magic and knew that the poor fool tried to make up for his lack of power with sheer bravado.

Quickly, Ethti, with Thomas standing beside her, outlined what they faced, telling them all about Eve, her location, and what she was trying to do.

"The council has met," Ethti said. "They are waiting to see if we can solve this problem before stepping in."

That caused a stir in the room. Ethti went on.

"We must stop the unicorn bleeding that Eve has planned for today. A City Knight will be watching every unicorn until this crisis is solved."

Dead silence.

Stunned silence. Just the idea of trying to guard that many unicorns had them shocked, but after Ethti's description of Eve, every one of them knew they would be no match for Eve's power.

Ethti smiled. "None of you are to attempt to stop Eve. Just report instantly that you have made contact with her or her human bleeder. We will stop her."

Ethti nodded to Thomas.

"Now get to the unicorns' locations as quickly as you can."

Behind Ethti, a map of the entire metropolitan area appeared on the wall, with a blue dot indicating the location of each unicorn. Over four hundred blue dots. Far more dots than the number of City Knights available to do the watching.

"Once you have made contact with a unicorn and have explained the situation, signal us and we will transport the unicorn to the Fantastics' holding apartments under the Met. We can protect them there. Then move on to the next closest unicorn. Understood?"

As one, everyone in the room nodded.

"And remember, do not engage Eve; only report to me instantly if you see her. I and others will jump there to help."

With that, Billie found herself back in Ethti's office, sitting back on the couch. A heck of a lot easier commute than the run she and Thomas had done before the meeting.

"Now we need your help, Squire," Ethti said, turning to her.

"Ready," Billie said, even though she had no idea exactly what Ethti was about to ask her to do.

"We don't dare let Eve get ahead of our Knights in this area. So we're going to divide up the unicorns in this area and the three of us are going to watch them until a Knight gets to each one."

"It's possible," Thomas said, breaking in before Billie could ask just how the heck she was supposed to watch over a hundred and forty-some different unicorns at the same time.

"Sure it is," Billie said, shaking her head.

"Trust me," Thomas said. "I will train you."

"Get it done," Ethti said, turning back to her desk.

Thomas sat beside Billie. "Go down your stairs to the platform of power and I'll explain it to you there."

"Okay, this I've got to hear." She closed her eyes, going down the staircase in her mind.

"I'm there," she said as she reached the landing.

As in their training sessions, Thomas's voice sounded like it was all around her. It sounded the same this time. "Now, Squire, open your remote viewing powers."

She imagined a case, like an old doctor's bag, with the words REMOTE VIEWING POWERS on the outside. Sometimes she used file cabinets to hold her spells, but for some reason she liked the idea of remote viewing powers being in an old doctor's bag. The bag was sitting on a shelf beside the platform. She took it down and opened it.

"Done."

"Inside is a special power of division. Pull that out now."

She reached into the dark insides of the black bag, smiling at the metaphor. Her imagined hand in the imagined bag felt a round, smooth object, which she pulled out and held up to the light. The object seemed to be a glass ball, only filled with hundreds of small squares.

"Got it," she said.

"Imagine it open and spreading in front of you like a map," Thomas said.

She did.

The ball opened, each mirror unfolding away from the rest until the entire ball became a flat frame full of small glass squares.

"Ain't that interesting," she said.

"Bring that image with you and open your eyes," Thomas said.

She did. The image of hundreds of small frames of glass now hung between her and Thomas like a window, fracturing his face into a whole bunch of tiny, yet still very attractive, parts. You couldn't do that to a lot of people's faces and still have them look good.

"Now search for a unicorn with your remote viewing," Thomas said. "Then place the running scene of the unicorn in one of the frames. Do the same for a second and a third and so on."

"Start with the Lower East Side and the Village," Ethti said. "Tell us when you are watching all the unicorns in that area."

Billie did as she had been told, finding a unicorn disguised as a teenage counter clerk in a bakery. She put the image on the first block in her square of glass images, watching it run for a moment as if it were on a small movie screen.

Then she found the second, a man standing on a corner waiting for a bus, and put the image of him in the second frame.

"Wow, split-screen television," Billie said, amazed that she could now watch two different scenes of daily life at once.

"It's working, I gather," Thomas said.

"I'll let you know after the first twenty," Billie said as she put a third image in the third square.

Less than five minutes later, she was watching the lives of one hundred and forty-seven unicorns pretending to be humans. And what was even more surprising, she could pay attention to all of them equally well, and talk to Thomas and Ethti at the same time.

She had always thought she had a one-track mind. Maybe she had in the past. It seemed that was no longer the case.

CHAPTER TWENTY-SEVEN

WHITEHEADS ON DARK SKIN

Thomas and Ethti had transported forty-one unicorns out of the locations Billie was watching to the safe area under the Metropolitan Museum. She was still keeping track of over a hundred unicorns when something started to go wrong on one of the tiny screens in her mind. It was as if a dark shadow had passed over it.

She sensed an evil presence looming near the unicorn. *Eve.*

"We have problems," Billie said. "Check it out for me. The unicorn in the back dining room of a restaurant on Sixth Avenue, just off Fortieth."

"Eve," Thomas said a moment later. "Ethti, connect with me. Follow my lead."

Thomas took Billie in an instant to the restaurant. The place smelled of baking bread. Billie realized it had been some time since breakfast.

Eve stood to one side as a human without magical powers worked to control the struggling unicorn. She turned to face them as they appeared.

Billie was shocked by the woman's appearance. She had imagined Eve as a dark presence when she had hovered around their table in the deli, but in person her skin was so dark that it shined in the dining room's faint light. She was tall, rail-thin, and at one time had been fashion-model pretty. Her long black hair flowed down over her back, almost touching her knees. She had on a striking white dress that left nothing to the imagination.

Billie's first thought was *Wow, she's striking*. Her second thought was *Man, who would want to look like that?*

Eve's magic shimmered around her, dark and thick, yet seemingly hollow. Billie didn't know what to make of that. Thomas's and Ethti's magic looked solid around them—with weak areas, but solid.

Eve's felt more like a balloon was containing her. A dark, evil balloon that could be popped.

"Ethti," Eve said, her voice too loud for the empty dining room. "Long time no see. Come to watch?"

Thomas, with a flick of his wrist, shoved the human away from the unicorn, smashing him into a wall. Billie was going to have to ask him later how he did that.

"Now, that wasn't very nice," Eve said, smiling at Thomas. "Snake Boy did nothing to you. All he wanted was a little blood."

Eve held out her hand and then started to close it, as if she were holding Thomas's throat from a distance.

Thomas went to the floor, choking.

"Don't you think you need to say you're sorry to Snake Boy?"

Then Eve, with her other hand, thrust at Ethti, taking her by the throat.

Ethti dropped to the ground next to Thomas.

"Now, dear Thomas," Eve said. "Say you're sorry before I kill you."

Billie could see the hole in Thomas's magic where Eve had thrust her hand. Ethti's magic looked only slightly damaged, but it was still unable to repel the choking hold.

Billie's first thought was to hit the woman with the shiny skin with a solid right punch. Then she remembered Thomas's words about fighting with her magic.

"No!" Billie shouted. "Not today. Not on my watch." Great Marine words, but in the back of a restaurant they sounded pretty hollow.

Eve just laughed.

Billie, in her mind, imagined that she took the magic black hands and yanked them away from Thomas and Ethti, just as she would have done in real life with real hands.

It worked!

Holy cow, now what?

Like a good marine, she decided that the best defense was a good offense. She stepped in front of the other two City Knights and faced Eve.

"Oh, we have a new one, with brand-new power," Eve said, laughing. "A simple, untrained squire, facing me. Adorable."

Billie had no idea what she was going to do, but she needed to give Thomas and Ethti a little time to recover.

Eve frowned. "I know you. You're the girl in the restaurant with Thomas. A little young, aren't you?"

Billie ignored Eve's laughter. Eve's magic was hollow. Hollow things could be punctured. Billie focused on forming a magical machine gun in her hands. A gun that fired magical bullets.

Hot bullets.

White-hot.

With luck, they would penetrate the black magic around Eve, puncture it the same way Eve's magic had punctured Thomas's and Ethti's shields.

"Silent type, I see," Eve said. "Well then, die in silence for all I care."

Eve was about to raise her hand to cast a spell when Billie fired, standing firm, the same way her Marine training had taught her to do, letting the shots flash to their target like a swarm of bees.

White, *hot* bees.

Eve staggered back slightly, but repelled all the shots. Suddenly Billie felt as if she were firing a pellet gun at a tank.

Then, beside her, Billie felt Ethti's presence, also firing a fantastical gun full of hot, white bullets.

Then Thomas joined them, also firing, taking up the image.

Eve screamed in pain and anger as some of the bullets got through and hit their mark, draining away some of her black energy, breaking down other areas, burning white marks into some of her dark skin.

White pimples on the perfectly dark skin.

Eve screamed some Marine-like language as she withered and swirled around, her long hair flying outward. She was losing the fight to avoid more of the hot bullets as Billie and Thomas and Ethti kept firing.

"Should I throw a bucket of water on her?" Billie asked.

"She won't melt," Thomas said.

"Bummer," Billie said.

The three of them stood there, firing, watching Eve do her jig.

"Intensify the energy in each bullet, Squire!" Ethti ordered.

Billie did as she was ordered, focusing as much power as she could into each hot bullet. She didn't have any idea how they might capture Eve, but for the moment more bullets would at least keep her busy until someone suggested a plan.

More white pimples appeared on Eve's black skin. She was going to need another entire can of black spray paint to cover these white marks. But nothing seemed to be doing any serious harm. A real person getting hit with that many real bullets would be bleeding from a thousand different wounds by now.

Billie kept firing, over and over, as if her gun were one of those magical movie weapons that never ran out of ammunition.

Thomas laughed softly. "That's got to hurt."

"Whiteheads always do," Billie said.

"You will pay for this!" Eve shouted, finally stopping her dance of evasion and facing the three of them. The bullets continued to puncture her magic and hit her. But Eve put up her hands and repelled some, somehow painting the once-white bullets black.

One caught Ethti in the shoulder.

Another caught Thomas in the leg.

A third caught Billie in the arm. The pain filled her mind; the gun in her hand vanished.

Then Eve was gone.

"Well done, Squire," Ethti said, holding her hand over the wound in her shoulder while she moved to make sure the unicorn was still alive.

"Yes, well done," Thomas said, waving a hand over his leg wound, making it vanish.

Billie dropped into a chair. She was bleeding like a stuck pig and she couldn't decide which hurt worse, the wound in her arm or the ache in her head.

Thomas moved over and brushed a hand over her wound and stopped the bleeding. Then he made a magic bandage appear over it. She could feel the injury beginning to heal already.

She put her head in her hands, hoping the pounding would stop. "Some aspirin and a nap might be nice right about now."

"The headache will pass," Thomas said.

"Can't capture her," Ethti said, helping the unicorn to its four feet. A moment later it was back inside its human form of a young waiter. "We should have been able to kill her with that onslaught."

"I'm glad I wasn't the only one who thought that," Billie said.

Thomas nodded. "Somehow we're going to have to kill her before this is over."

"How?" Billie asked, daring to look up. "I doubt my little make-believe machine gun is going to work a second time without killing everyone and everything around her."

Thomas shrugged and rubbed his throat where the imprint of a woman's hand still showed red and sore. Suddenly, the imprint vanished as if it had never been there. He sure had a healing touch.

"So what do we do now?" Billie asked.

"We gather up Snake Boy and—"

Thomas turned to where he had thrown the tattooed man against the wall. Snake Boy was gone.

"Eve must have taken him," Ethti said.

"No, she didn't," the unicorn waiter said. "The guy with the snake tattoos staggered out the side door when you were fighting with the dark sorceress."

"Thank you," Ethti said. "Medical attention is waiting for you."

At that, Ethti transported the unicorn to safety.

"We can't let Snake Boy get back to Eve," Thomas said. "She needs a human to do the draining for her ritual. She has him trained, so she needs him today."

"We have a short period before she thinks to look for him," Ethti said. "First she's going to try to heal some of her wounds."

"Good," Thomas said.

"So, let's get Snake Boy back," Billie said.

"You two search for him," Ethti said. "I'll alert the rest of the world to put watches on as many unicorns as they can. She's not going to try for a second unicorn in this area."

"I suggest you finish rounding them up anyway," Thomas said. "Better to be safe."

Ethti nodded. "I agree." Then she was gone.

Thomas quickly went to the spot where he had tossed Snake Boy and put a trace spell on the site. A blue line lit up, floating in the air. The line went out the door.

"Can you see that, Squire?"

"Like a blue ribbon headed for a prize," Billie said, pushing herself to her feet.

The wound on her arm ached, but not enough to stop her.

A moment later, they stepped onto the brightly lit street. The light stabbed into her head like a sword and she had to stop for a moment and let her eyes adjust slowly.

A block away, a crowd had gathered, filling the street from building to building. Music drifted over parked cars, along with laughter.

The blue trace line disappeared right into the crowd.

Damn.

Billie glanced up and remembered what was scheduled for today, one day ahead of Halloween, because some president or prime minister was touring the city the next day. The Halloween parade. The streets were already filling up with revelers whose wild costumes and makeup would make the tattoo-ridden Snake Boy look like a pasty-faced stockbroker commuting back to the suburbs after work. For once, the little freak would blend right in.

Even with a trace spell, finding him before Eve did just got a lot harder.

CHAPTER TWENTY-EIGHT

NOT YOUR EVERYDAY SOUSA

It had been a long week, chock-full of unicorns, elves, dwarfs, dragons, fairies, sorceresses, and the like. As an ex-marine—and, perhaps more important, as a native New Yorker—Billie didn't shock easily. But, then, this was the first time she'd ever been in the Village on the night of the Halloween parade.

The blue trace line tracking Snake Boy twisted through crowds of men dressed as Nurse Betty, women dressed as Rambo, and enough drag queens to deplete the East Coast of its entire supply of feather boas.

The sidewalks on both sides of the street were jammed with onlookers, many of whom skipped and ran along beside the parade, blurring the lines between audience and participants.

Snake Boy had gone upstream, against the flow of the crowd.

As she and Thomas rushed into the crowd, a band consisting of men dressed like Dorothy from *The Wizard of Oz*, ruby slippers and all, broke into a rousing rendition of "Somewhere Over the Rainbow" while high-stepping slowly as if they were trying to cross a field full of cow shit.

Billie glanced at them, then turned quickly away. Some of them should have worn underwear under their skirts. Maybe they just forgot. Yeah, right.

Thomas looked pale and flustered as he tried to follow the blue line, pushing people aside with as much politeness as his Englishness could muster.

"I hate this parade," Thomas said.

"American tradition."

"As I have always said, you Americans are a really strange bunch."

At that moment, a man wearing a Tinker Bell outfit and a two-sizes-too-small diaper blocked their way.

"Isn't this just *marvelous*," he said in a rumbling construction-worker voice. Then he sprinkled fairy dust on Thomas before moving on.

"You don't see this type of thing where I'm from," her mentor huffed, trying to brush off the sparkles and mostly failing.

Billie burst out laughing. "Oh please. I've seen *Benny Hill*. And I'll wager you've seen plenty of Shakespeare. When it premiered."

Thomas just frowned. *Colonists one, Redcoats zero*, Billie thought with smug satisfaction.

A tall, blond woman gave a bloodcurdling war cry next to Thomas. She was wearing a hard hat, high heels, and overalls with the straps covering parts of her chest.

She stepped in front of Thomas, lowered her shoulder, and opened a path through the crowd the way a marine would, shoving ahead, following the blue line tracing

Snake Boy's path. The fate of the world was at stake. A few bruised shoulders would be a small price to pay to save it.

After a half block of getting whacked by men's purses and tripped by long skirts on poodles, Billie stopped, stepped into an alcove, and pulled Thomas with her. They were both breathing hard.

"He's got too much of a head start through this crowd," she shouted over a ragtime number played on kazoos by a group of women dressed in matching men's business suits and carrying briefcases. "We have to get to him before Eve comes back and finds him. Any ideas?"

He shook his head.

"How about you jump us a block ahead, see if we can pick up the trail?"

Instantly she knew the answer to that. If Thomas jumped, the tracking would be broken and the blue line would vanish. If that happened, they would lose him in these crowds for sure.

"It would break—"

"I remember."

Thomas glanced around. "I'll keep following the trail. Do you think you could remote-view ahead to see if you could find him? If you do, I'll jump to him and call for you to join me."

"I think I can do that," Billie said.

With a frown at two drag queens dressed in flowing Queen Victoria gowns, crowns and all, Thomas plunged back into the crowd.

Billie leaned against the building and tried to get up enough energy to do a remote viewing spell. Her arm ached where her own magical bullet had come back to hit her. Luckily, it hadn't got her between the eyes.

She focused on the remote spell, letting her mind roam ahead of Thomas over the crowd. She could no longer see the blue line, but she did have an aerial view, which was better than having to paw her way through the middle of the crush.

There were a lot of New Yorkers dressed in regular street clothes watching the parade, and a fair number of police. Almost everyone was either standing still or moving with the flow of the parade, so she tried to focus her mind on anything moving against it.

Finally she spotted Snake Boy, pushing his way through a herd of Norman Bateses all chanting, "Coming, Mother!"

She found Thomas and transported herself as close to him as she could get.

Suddenly she was there, right in front of Snake Boy, filling an empty spot between two drag queens in beautiful gowns.

"Going somewhere?" Thomas asked.

Snake Boy stopped cold, looking very afraid.

"Where did you come from, little thing?" one of the drag queens asked Billie.

"He's going nowhere with you," Eve said to Thomas as she appeared beside Snake Boy.

She wrapped her charge in a protective bubble of dark force as Thomas put up his shield and Billie joined hers with his.

"Oh, a show," one drag queen said, clapping his hands like a little girl getting a present.

"Nice outfit," a drag queen said to Eve. Then he seemed to notice all the white dots. "You know, honey, there's a fabulous dermatologist on the Upper West Side who could give you something for that."

"Her insurance won't cover it," Billie said.

Oh, the drag queen mouthed sympathetically.

Eve glared at Billie. "One more night and you will pay for what you have done."

"Not as much as you're gonna pay if you don't get some decent insurance," said the drag queen with a toss of her blond-bewigged head.

Thomas reached out and struck at Eve with an intense bolt of energy.

Eve staggered slightly, but then just smiled.

Thomas was keeping Eve busy for the moment, so Billie knew it was up to her to deal with Snake Boy. They needed to take at least that much away from Eve to slow her down.

She had to hold Snake Boy right where he was.

Hold spell.

That would do it. It had been one of the spells that Thomas had taught her in their last training session.

Eve fired back at Thomas, but this time Thomas's screen seemed to hold. Maybe the white bullets had weakened her a little.

"Nice try," Thomas said. "But you're never quite strong enough, are you, love?"

Billie used the distraction to open a tiny hole in Eve's spell with a hot white knife, then through the hole wrapped a hold spell on the bottom of Snake Boy's feet and around his ankles. It all took only a fraction of a second. Unless Eve was even more powerful than Billie suspected and could take with her most of the concrete in a city block, Snake Boy wasn't going anywhere.

Eve struck again, but again Thomas didn't move. He just stood there and laughed.

With a wave of her hand, Eve vanished.

And most of Snake Boy vanished.

Most.

Billie stared at the two tennis shoes, dirty white socks, and bare legs left sitting on the sidewalk, bleeding slightly from all the ripped flesh around the knees.

A half dozen queens around them stared for a moment.

"Well, that's disgraceful. You can't just leave that poor boy that way," said the tallest of the group. "Someone at least get him a decent pair of pumps." Billie, the tough ex-marine, just stood there. She felt like crying.

Chapter Twenty-nine

SEND BACK
THE BLEEDER

The scream coming from Snake Boy was just too much. It seemed to go on and on as he stared at where his legs used to be, and at his pumping blood spurting all over the cave floor.

Eve muffled the sound, trying to decide if it was worth doing anything. Or if there was anything she could do. The young, stupid squire would pay for this, and pay dearly.

Snake Boy took another breath, screamed again, lay back, and passed out.

"Good," Eve said, unmuffling the sound around her.

She could go back and get his legs, put them back on his feet with a mend spell, but he still wouldn't be in good enough shape to help her bleed a unicorn today. Either way, she was going to have to find another human to do the task for tonight's ritual. And for tomorrow's finale as well.

Also, if she tried to save Snake Boy, she would have to face Thomas again, and she just wasn't ready to do that. The day had drained her. But one more night of power would be enough to shut her ex-husband's rude mouth permanently.

"Sorry," she said to Snake Boy. With a wave of her hand, she sent him back to the sidewalk where his legs were. Let the goody-goody types in the City Knights try to save him if they wanted. It no longer mattered to her.

But what did matter was her skin, and what Thomas, Ethti, and that squire had done to her with those white bullets.

Eve moved to the mirror in her bedroom area and stared at her skin. What had been perfect black beauty was now scarred by white points. Hundreds of them. And they seemed to be growing slowly instead of shrinking, as if her old skin was trying to come back to the surface.

Tonight, that would change.

Tonight, she would stay in the stream longer than any other night, take in even more power. The white dots would vanish then forever. And no one would be powerful enough to even touch her, especially her idiot ex-husband.

"First things first," she said, turning away from the mirror and moving back to the main area of the cave, where the faded drawing covered the cave floor.

She needed more unicorn blood.

She needed a human under her control to get it for her. And not just any human would do. It had to be someone who liked to kill, loved the idea of blood draining from a living creature. Most humans would just pass out at the sight.

Snake Boy had been special. Where could she find someone like him?

Then it dawned on her.

A moment later she was walking the corridors of Attica, with men whistling at her slinky, revealing white dress and her beautiful body.

They adored her.

They wanted her.

Soon every person on the planet would feel the same way.

CHAPTER THIRTY

THE LAST DAY OF A UNICORN ROUNDUP

Stunned at what she had done, Billie released her hold spell on Snake Boy's shoes and legs. One leg remained upright; the other fell over with a faint plopping sound. Blood drained out onto the sidewalk.

She wanted to be sick.

An instant later, Snake Boy's body appeared on the sidewalk beside his legs. Thomas instantly sprang into action. With a quick spell, he took all three parts of Snake Boy, plus Billie, and flashed them to the medical area of City Knights headquarters.

Billie found herself shoved to one side of the white emergency room as doctors and nurses, all wizards and sorceresses specializing in medical magic, worked over Snake Boy.

Within thirty seconds the team had his legs attached, and thirty seconds after that, new blood was flowing through him.

Within two minutes they moved away, nodding and talking to themselves, letting Snake Boy rest.

All Billie could do was stand there watching, stunned beyond any words. She had killed two Red Guard in Iraq during the invasion. And even though she knew that Snake Boy had been the one who had killed the unicorn she saw, maybe more unicorns than that, she was just stunned at how a simple misuse of her magic had caused all this.

Now, much too late, she understood. While they worked on Snake Boy, she had gone deeper into the spell, seeing its limitations. Holding a human by the feet while someone else was pulling hard on another part was not a good idea. The human body was just too easy to rip apart.

Way too easy.

"He's going to live," Thomas said, moving over beside Billie. "You going to be all right?"

"No," she said. "I didn't understand how my power could be used."

"You will, Squire, given enough decades and centuries. No one knows it all. There's just too much."

Billie shook her head. "Centuries? I *wish* I had that much time."

"Oh, you do," Thomas said, resting a hand on her shoulder. "In fact, with your level of power, there's no telling how long you're going to live. No one has really done a study."

"Oh, sure," she said. But deep in her training, deep in the hours she had spent down on her magic platform in her mind, she knew she had learned that was the case. She was going to live a very long time. If . . . She decided to say the rest out loud. "If Eve doesn't kill us all first."

"Well, there is that," Thomas said. "Let's go see how the unicorn roundup is doing."

Billie nodded and a moment later they were standing in Ethti's office. The giant map had very few dots left on it. As Billie watched, two more vanished.

"Good work," Ethti said, turning to face Billie. "And thank you, Squire."

Billie could only nod. No matter how much Thomas talked, she still knew she had made a mistake. And she was going to make more, since she was so new at this. Knowing that was a bad thing. The one thing they had drilled into her in Marine combat training was that hesitation got you killed. If she couldn't clear out the worry about making a mistake, she might hesitate in the coming fight with Eve.

"We've got most of the local unicorns contained and protected," Ethti said.

"Worldwide?" Thomas asked.

"The council has issued an alert and all City Knights are moving as many unicorns as they can into protective custody. But there are over one hundred thousand unicorns scattered over the world."

Over one hundred thousand? Billie had no idea there were that many.

"We're not going to be able to protect them all," Thomas said. "But at least Snake Boy's capture has slowed Eve down some."

Suddenly Ethti seemed distant, as if she was listening to something. Then she said, "I wouldn't count on it. There has been a problem today at Attica."

Billie instantly knew what had happened. You need to shop for a cold-blooded killer, go to where they're kept stacked up.

"It was reported that a woman with a skin problem, wearing a slinky white dress, appeared in a cell of the prison, then vanished with a convict."

"Who did she take?" Billie asked.

"Samuel Blythe-Wallace," Ethti said. A picture of a meek-looking accountant type appeared on Ethti's desk.

"Better known as Payday Sam," Billie said. "Convicted of cutting open three women and leaving them to die. He is also suspected of many other killings, all using knives. Loves to cut things, mostly women. A master with any type of blade."

Billie dropped onto Ethti's couch, suddenly feeling the tiredness of days of no sleep. All that they had done today hadn't slowed Eve down at all. Just marked her and made her even more angry. Now Eve had at her side one of the state's most notorious killers. And tonight, if she found a unicorn to bleed somewhere in the world, she would gain even more power, release even more hallows onto the city, cause more destruction.

And tomorrow night, if they couldn't stop her, the world might very well end.

"Thinking happy thoughts, Squire?" Thomas asked as he stood beside Billie in front of the huge map that Ethti had just magically plastered on the front wall of the Big Meeting Room. It was ablaze with bright yellow dots showing the locations of unguarded unicorns around the world. There were too many to count.

Billie looked at her partner as if he were nuts, then laughed. "More like fantasies."

Thomas's smile faded. He shot her a nervous sidelong glance and cleared his throat. Uh-oh. A quick explanation was in order, or he might have a heart attack. Englishmen. Jeez.

"What I'm trying to say is, I wish we could figure out how to speed up this process somehow. It'd take years to reach every unicorn if we had to keep notifying them one at a time. I mean, damn, if you just do the math, it's downright alarming."

"Alarming . . ." Ethti repeated thoughtfully.

"Yeah, as in scary," Billie said, but her superiors were no longer listening. They were just looking at one another, smiling. Billie wondered what she had missed.

"If we simply combine our powers, then we can just put alarms on all of them at once. It could work. Good plan, Squire," Thomas said.

One thing the Marines had taught her was to accept credit when a superior gave it to you. Even if you didn't think you deserved it.

"Thanks, uh, I guess that's what comes from thinking those happy thoughts."

"Not happy enough, I'm afraid." Ethti frowned as she turned from the map to face them both.

"Don't get me wrong, Squire. Alarms are a good start."

Billie heard a "but" coming.

"But it's not enough to notify the unicorns. We also have to get them to safety." And there it was: a big, fat "but."

When Billie asked why they couldn't just gallop off to a safe haven by *themselves*, she got a puzzling answer. Thomas explained that the unicorns wouldn't necessarily bow to the will of the City Knights, even if it was in their best interests to do so. They would listen only to their king, and no one knew where he was. Apparently he hadn't supported the Great Treaty and went into hiding shortly after it took effect. So it all boiled down to politics, and a five-thousand-year-old grudge.

Happy thoughts indeed.

CHAPTER THIRTY-ONE

TOO LATE

"First things first," Ethti had said, which was why Thomas and Billie got right to work on the spell to attach alarms to the unicorns. Even if there wasn't enough time for a wild-goose chase—or was it more of a wild-horse chase?—after the Unicorn King, even if the unicorns wouldn't listen to an alert from any source other than their own leader, City Knights had to warn them anyway. "It's what we do," Ethti had said.

Billie had just closed her eyes and started to focus when word came in that another unicorn had been found, dead and bled in southern France. No time to perfect their spell now. Thomas told her they would have to just go with what they had. Billie rolled her shoulders and tried to relax.

The spell seemed slow at first, even though she had no real-world time frame to measure the slowness with. But the feeling in her mind of slowness soon changed as the process became more and more automatic. Faster and faster she went, the unicorns a blur in her mind. She didn't even pay attention to what part of the world she was in. She just set the spell and automatically jumped to the next unicorn, like a spark leaping between two posts.

Set the spell and leap.

Set the spell and leap.

The spell wasn't as draining as she had expected. Thomas had to be giving her some sort of power boost. On top of that, it was a small spell that took very little energy to set or maintain. Didn't compare to making up machine guns with magic bullets to fire at a dark sorceress.

Suddenly, the entire process just stopped.

She felt as if she had been riding in a bus and the driver had slammed on the brakes.

For a moment she looked for a new target, feeling as if she had more than enough energy to continue, but her mind would not find the next unguarded unicorn for her.

Maybe Thomas had stopped her. A sudden panic grabbed her. She needed help from him right now, to figure out what had just happened.

She opened her eyes.

Thomas and Ethti both stood with their backs to her, staring at the world map.

Every light on the map was green.

She had done the *entire* planet, every unicorn, all by herself. She would know instantly if any unicorn was in danger from this moment forward.

"Now, sister, *that* was impressive," an old man's voice behind her said. The voice had a Brooklyn accent.

She turned around to stare for a moment into the swirling colors of two massive unicorn eyes floating in midair.

Then the eyes were gone.

"Amazing," Thomas said, still facing the map of the world. "I would have never thought it possible." Ethti nodded in agreement.

Billie just kept staring at the empty space in the Big Meeting Room where the huge unicorn eyes had been. Then she asked, "Did anyone else hear that?"

CHAPTER THIRTY-TWO

DREAMS OF FLIGHT

The dreams were shattering.

Rallidae, the Great Bird King, soared over the vast green lands and the deep blue oceans, controlling all that he saw. No one dared stand against him. Everyone worshipped him.

Where his droppings landed became shrines where flowers grew and the young played.

Where he stopped to eat became holy ground, revered for decades, the fruit sacred, to be eaten only by the most faithful of his followers.

He rested only on the tallest peaks, or at the tops of the largest cliffs, where he could overlook his lands, see his people, revel in their worship of him.

His were the ways of a great king. A powerful ruler.

He was that ruler.

No one held the power that he held.

But lately, while resting on his mountain perches, his dreams had become rancid and broken. He often found himself rolling in the foulest-smelling mud, with creatures around him that screamed as he smashed them.

Nightmares. Not the dreams of soaring a great king should have.

But he could not discover where the nightmares came from.

His beautiful feathers would turn to scaly skin in his nightmares, and the unthinkable also happened as he found himself tired, falling to the ground, with no one there to help him.

No one to help their king.

In some of the worst of the dark visions, the Unicorn King, the great white wingless creature with no name, stood against him, driving him and his followers to the ground.

Below the ground.

The nightmare was so real that it felt almost like a memory.

Yet his great magic would not allow him to find the truth of the dream, or stop the nightmares.

Nightmare to soaring back to nightmare.

Again and again.

His sleep had not always been this way. With his power, with the legions of beings that followed and worshipped him, it should *not* be this way.

Yet the nightmare of rolling in the slime, of smelling the stink, returned again and again. The Unicorn King's rainbow eyes taunted him, yet he felt too tired to strike back.

This was not a sleep he was enjoying.

If the good dreams did not return and remain, he would be forced to discover who was responsible for the disturbance.

If he had to lay waste to entire parts of the world to discover his tormentor, he would do so. His sleep was important to him.

It was important to any ruler.

CHAPTER THIRTY-THREE

BRING IN THE DRUGS, PLEASE

The lady was simply certifiably insane, crazier than anything Samuel had ever seen, and he had seen many seriously sick things over the years. He had committed a few insane acts himself as well. At least, that's what everyone told him. He didn't consider the acts insane; they were just a form of release for him.

But in all his years, he hadn't seen anything resembling this slinky lady who spray-painted herself in dark colors and wore white dresses. Somehow she had gotten him out of Attica and had him kill and bleed a small pony he thought had been a woman when he started. Now, killing a woman was one thing. Killing a pony, that was just nuts. Far beyond the pale. It had made him sick to his stomach.

Actually, he had believed for the longest time that he had never left Attica, that he had just gone on a head trip, not a real trip.

Drugs maybe?

He had no memory of ingesting anything, or being stuck by any drug-carrying instrument.

Maybe he had just finally lost it. This place could do that to a guy.

Then again, perhaps not. He felt in complete control of his mind and body. Yet, he had to admit, one moment he was in his cell reliving a wonderful memory of slashing a brunette's throat, and the next the Spray-Painted Lady was standing in front of him.

Fact: The cell door had not opened.

Fact: He had not left his cell.

And Lefty still snored on the bunk above, so he doubted her appearance was his doing.

For a moment after her arrival, Samuel had stared up at her, wondering if she had been someone he had killed. Granted, he couldn't remember them all, but he didn't think she was. He was sure he would have re-membered a woman with shiny dark paint all over her.

Besides, she was too tall. He liked his women his height. Easier to cut their throats when he was finished. Tall women he had to reach up to do that, and he hated feeling short.

So the woman staring down at him in his cell wasn't some ghost bothering him. Therefore, logically, he had to be drugged. It was the only explanation, so he just went with that.

He was a man who needed everything in order. They said he looked and acted like an accountant, which was also why the press had called him Payday Sam, a name he despised. He had never done a payroll in his life, al-though he did like numbers. He knew the exact number of buttons on the white blouses of every one of his women. He always had them put on white blouses before he slit their throats. The blood showed up better that way.

"Samuel Blythe-Wallace?" she asked, leaning down and smiling at him. Her black eyes seemed to light up the lower bunk more than his reading lamp did.

"At your service," he said, standing and giving her a slight bow. He figured he might as well play along with the drugs. Always easier than fighting them.

The sound of his answer must have woken up Lefty.

Lefty seldom showered and often smelled of old vomit, a truly unpleasant odor late at night.

He snorted, rolled over with a grump, then said, "Oh, wow, baby!"

"You can see her?" Samuel asked, not expecting his cellmate to play a part in his drug-induced hallucination.

Lefty licked his lips, swung his legs over the edge of his mattress, and started to get down from his bunk. "Hoping to do a little more than just seeing. What do you say, baby? Just a little—"

He didn't make it off his bunk. With a flick of her wrist, moving far faster than Samuel could see, she shoved Lefty back against the concrete wall so hard his head cracked like a bad egg. His eyes went blank as the life drained out of him, a look Samuel had seen many times in his women.

"I should be worshipped, not slobbered over," she said.

"You know, I'm going to get blamed for that."

She laughed. "It won't matter. I'm giving you a job of a lifetime. All you have to do is kill a few things. I assume that will not be a problem for you?"

Before he could answer, he was next to a woman who looked like she was in her mid-twenties. The three of them were standing in an odd sort of living room that seemed somehow smaller and fussier than those of his previous victims.

The woman started swearing at them in French, demanding that they leave at once.

"Kill her," the Spray-Painted Lady said. She handed him a very nice knife, one that looked ancient and well used. "Put her blood in this."

She held up a large glass decanter that looked like it had been made for fine wine, not for holding blood.

The woman of the house looked like she was trying to run, but her feet were stuck to the floor. She started to scream, but her voice was cut off.

"And if I decline?" Samuel asked.

"I will break your neck, return you to your cell, and find another to kill for me."

Samuel had no doubt that the woman would do exactly as she said she would do. And drug hallucination or not, there was no point in fighting her.

"It seems you have found yourself an employee."

She smiled. "Good."

He bowed again, then took the offered knife. "Is there a ritual you would like me to perform? I have my own, but I doubt it would be something you would care to watch."

"Just get as much blood into the jar as possible. Every drop is important."

He had done as he was told, enjoying the kill until halfway through the draining of the blood. The woman suddenly turned into a pony with a horn attached to its head like some make-believe unicorn creature.

It put him right off. He killed women, not ponies. At that moment, he wished the hallucination, or nightmare, or whatever he was in, would stop. Maybe the prison was trying a new type of treatment on him.

He finished the task she had assigned, pony or not.

"Wipe all blood off the outside of the glass, then give it to me."

He did that as well.

For a moment, she held up the flask full of blood as if she had found gold; then, with a laugh, she waved an arm and the two of them were in a cavelike place. Colder than the house and a lot larger.

"You have done well," she said to him.

He smiled. "Thank you."

She pointed to a small nook in the rock. "Stand there and watch until I tell you otherwise. I will need your help again. If you serve me well, you will be rewarded beyond your wildest dreams."

"I have very wild dreams," he said.

She smiled. He knew at that moment just how insane she was. "How about as many women as you would like, without any chance of repercussions?"

He smiled back at her. "I accept your terms." He turned and moved to the place she had indicated, then turned and faced her, standing like a guard in front of Buckingham Palace.

"We may have a very long relationship," the woman said, nodding, clearly pleased with him. Then she went to work carefully pouring out the blood onto a pattern on the stone.

It wasn't until five minutes later, when he tried to adjust his stance, that he realized he couldn't move his feet. Two hours later, he was starting to wish the drugs would wear off, and beginning to worry that they wouldn't.

CHAPTER THIRTY-FOUR

STICK A CORK IN IT

Billie felt stupid. First she got blank stares from Thomas and Ethti when she told them about the unicorn eyes, and now she was getting multiple blank stares from a roomful of City Knights because she had asked a question. A stupid question.

Well, what else could they reasonably expect from her? She was new, and dirty, and smelly, and sleep-deprived; her query probably hadn't made any sense. Still, even if it was a stupid question, Billie thought it deserved an answer. She took a deep breath and tried to rephrase. "Okay, so we can't break through the defensive screens around Eve's cave, right?" Ethti nodded patiently. "So how do the black power and the hallows coming up from Rallidae get in and out? I must be missing something, right?" More silence. But then Thomas smiled, and so did Ethti. Soon, most of the room was grinning, except for Austin, of course.

"Squire," Ethti said, "in your basic ignorance, you might well have given us a solution."

"Thanks," Billie said. "I think."

"It's perfect," Thomas said. "We plug up the escape hole and it will flood her cavern with the hallows while she's trying to concentrate on the spell."

"It wouldn't hold her or the hallows for long," Ethti said. "Once she shut off the power flow from Rallidae and stepped out of the pattern, she would be able to deal with the problem. But it might cause her to shut it off sooner."

"Why?" Billie asked.

"Why what, Squire?" Thomas asked.

Billie wasn't sure what she was talking about, but she decided to just go ahead and blurt out her ignorance.

"Why wouldn't it be possible to put a more powerful containment spell around her cavern at the same time, so she can't just move them out?"

That silence again.

Thomas nodded. "We should be able to use the same containment spells to hold her in that she's using to keep us out. We could get other City Knights and some of the council to help us make it very, very strong. Given enough time, we could build it to hold her for all time."

"If we block the extra magic coming from Rallidae," Ethti said, "and feed it back into her cave and hold it there, it might even kill her. Or at the very least trap her."

Silence for a third time again in the Big Meeting Room.

Billie just wanted to rest. Maybe her ideas hadn't been that stupid. Maybe they would let her go get some sleep now.

Thomas laughed, the wonderful sound filling up the Big Meeting Room.

Ethti looked at him with a frown.

"Just think about it," he said. "After what she's done, the idea of her ruling over a cave full of evil hallows for all eternity seems like just punishment to me."

"Do you say that about all your ex-wives?" Billie asked.

"Only some of them," Thomas said.

CHAPTER THIRTY-FIVE

BAD DRAINAGE
CAN BE GOOD

Thomas led the spell, but Billie wasn't the only other participant. Every New York–based City Knight plus twenty-three of the most powerful wizards and sorceresses on the planet leaned back in their chairs, closed their eyes, and held hands.

Billie could sense others as well. Many others. Far more than were in the room physically.

She could see through Thomas's eyes what he was seeing as his presence hovered in the rock below Eve's cave, waiting for the power to arrive.

Suddenly, it was as if a black stream of dark oil was shooting up from below.

Thomas wrapped all of Eve's containment spell and cave in an entrapment spell of his own, leaving only the opening where the dark stream entered.

Billie put all her energy with his, adding to his spell, adding strength where she sensed weakness.

Let me draw from your power. Thomas's thought was as clear as a bell to her

Take what you need.

She felt herself open up, felt something draining from her like the feeling of a wound bleeding.

Others were either giving Thomas power as well or forming their own shields, layer after layer of entrapment spells, all entwined with each other, helping each other.

It felt weird to Billie. She could see exactly what was happening, as if she were watching it all on a movie screen. Yet at the same time she knew she was in the Big Meeting Room and also floating with Thomas.

Weird, very weird.

So, would what Thomas had done turn back the energy stream?

And then, would it hold the new power of Eve?

The area where the black stream was stopped and turned back suddenly felt weak. Billie watched as Thomas went to it at once, adding strength.

Others added thickness.

Ethti, always a picture of calm and power, seemed to be directing traffic, helping Thomas lead the fight.

Billie could feel the power of the others.

Some were as strong as Thomas, some weren't.

The power from inside the cave felt like a pressure pushing outward, ready to burst at any moment. The black energy wanted out, but they weren't going to let it.

More City Knights from around the world joined in the fight, adding layers of spells upon layers of spells.

Suddenly, the black stream from far below shut off.

Thomas and a hundred other City Knights instantly snapped the hole closed, rounding their containment shields, using the fullness of the shape to add even more strength.

Layer and anchor the containment spells to the rock. Let the spells take energy from the earth itself.

For a moment, Billie thought she could hear Eve screaming inside the cave. Or maybe she had just imagined how angry Eve would be, and wanted her to scream and fight.

As long as Ethti and Thomas and the City Knights won.

CHAPTER THIRTY-SIX

HOME, HALLOW, HOME

Eve spread her arms high over her head, letting the dark energy flow over her naked body like a soothing summer wind. The damage to her skin healed almost instantly, erasing the white marks as if they had never been there. She could feel her power and strength growing by the second.

It felt fantastic, like the best, most soothing shower she had ever taken.

A half dozen ancient hallows flashed past her in the energy stream. She planned on being in the stream far longer than before, and spreading the hallows out over an area covering three states. It would be so much fun watching those fool City Knights chase them all.

"Excuse me, O Supreme Dark Witch of the South, or whatever you are."

She had told Payday Sam to stand in the corner and say nothing. He was free to watch, and if he notified her when eight minutes had gone by, he would be rewarded. But he wasn't supposed to interrupt her for any reason before that.

She kept her eyes closed, her arms stretched toward the ceiling, taking in the power.

"Houston, I believe we have a problem," Sam said.

She ignored him again.

"Wake up, you imbecile!" Sam shouted.

She gritted her teeth. He had just sealed his death as far as she was concerned.

"Look around you. I'm fairly certain this isn't what you were planning."

She opened her eyes to a scene of total chaos. A hundred ancient hallows were scattering around her cave. Ten of them stood around her, pointing at her wonderful body and snickering like fools.

The entire room echoed with the remains of the energy as it bounced around inside her cave like a wind filled with soot, turning everything pure black, including Payday Sam.

She looked up through the stream of energy. Something was blocking its exit.

City Knights.

She could sense Thomas and Ethti and the council, their spells surrounding her cave. How dare they do this to her?

Her anger flared as she gave the spell to cut off the energy coming from below. They would pay dearly for what they had done. Death would be too easy for them. They deserved much, much worse now.

The stream of energy finally stopped, and she stepped naked toward the hallows surrounding her. One reached out to touch her and lost its hand for the effort.

The rest dropped back.

Everything was pitch black, as even her lights had been covered with the sootlike energy spell. She spelled more lights into existence and locked them to the ceiling, then glanced around. She was shocked at the hundreds of ancient hallows that seemed to fill every inch of her cave.

"You might consider giving these creatures a bath," Payday Sam said. "They smell worse than the toilets in a holding cell for drunks."

"In good time," she said. She would take care of them soon enough. Right now, she had to break through the spell surrounding her cave and teach those City Knights a well-deserved lesson.

She spelled herself a new dress, then stood and took stock of how she felt. Never in all her life had she been as strong, as magic-filled as she was right at that moment.

She did a quick check of the entrapment spell in place around her cave. The City Knights had done well, locking the spell into the rocks, closing off the hole where the energy had come in the moment she stopped it. At her old magic levels, she would have never been able to break through.

But now she was a black sorceress, a power that would rise from the ground and strike down anyone who dared oppose her.

She laughed, the sound echoing even over the chatter of the ancient hallows.

"Glad you think this is funny," Payday Sam said as two hallows stripped the last of his clothes off him.

She put a quick protect spell around him. He was going to die an ugly death for what he had called her, but at the moment she still needed him alive to bleed one or two more unicorns.

She imagined the hottest, sharpest, most intense cutting spell she knew, then put all her power behind it and aimed it at the entrapment spell surrounding her cave. Her power would cut through their spell like a sharpened butcher's knife through a lover's skin.

She would then move to the surface and spread the hallows in her cave over the city.

CHAPTER THIRTY-SEVEN

MAD EVE

Thomas kept warning them to expect an attack from Eve at any moment.

Billie knew it was going to happen.

Everyone did.

But the intensity of the blow still stunned Billie when it hit.

Concentrated in one place on the interwoven spells, a sharp, daggerlike force fought to break through, jabbing at the magic shields with a razor-sharp point.

Billie felt a couple of the weaker wizards break away from the group in agony.

Billie felt her own head threaten to explode in pain, or at least that's what it felt like. The attack drove spikes into Billie's mind. It was like the worst migraine she had ever had.

Doubled.

Hold on!

Even through the pain and searing heat of Eve's counterattack, Thomas's thoughts sounded calm and in control.

Cooling.

Billie fought back, giving as much of her power to Thomas as she could as he tried to hold the spells together with the sheer force of his will. He was taking the brunt of the attack because he was the strongest.

She wanted to scream at the pain, run away from it. But no marine ever ran away from anything.

This was war.

Even though she wasn't fighting with fists and guns, this was what she had been trained to do.

She poured even more of her energy into Thomas.

She ignored the pain, pushed it aside as if it didn't matter, forced herself to stand behind Thomas, trying to give him all the support she could.

He focused as much force as he could at the spells holding the containment area. Over the one point of Eve's direct attack, Thomas seemed to be building a thick, steel-like patch.

It was holding, from what she could tell through the heat and pain flooding her mind.

But Eve seemed to be concentrating more and more power on the single point.

Thomas sent more and more of his energy, and those backing him, at that point. Billie knew, could sense, that this was the moment: The fate of the world rested on what happened right here, right now.

The hot force from inside suddenly stopped. The pain vanished, an echo wrapped into a memory. She was going to have one amazing headache, that was for sure.

For the moment, Thomas and all the rest had held Eve.

For the moment. Eve might not have used her full power. Billie hoped she had, but she might not have.

Frantically, every wizard and sorceress kept going, layering in more spells, more containment balls intertwined with the early ones, all tied to the rocks and earth for power.

She will try again. Thomas's thought rang through everyone's minds, warning them to stay ready.

An instant later, the attack came again.

Again Billie wanted to scream out in pain as the searing-hot attack seemed to rip at every cell in her body.

Somehow, somewhere deep inside, she knew that marines didn't cry out in pain. They gritted their teeth and fought through the pain, won the fight, won the war.

She would hold, give Thomas everything she had, if it killed her.

Thomas pushed back, using a mirror spell Billie didn't even realize she knew anything about until she saw it. He wove it into the containment fields to reverse some of the force and shove it back at Eve.

The attack stopped again.

Keep building. Thomas seemed cool and calm.

Billie had no idea how he could be calm under the circumstances. She felt drained, beaten-up, punished, and she had been behind him, just helping him.

Again, Eve attacked, thrusting smaller thrusts, as if jabbing at them.

Thomas stayed with each thrust, instantly throwing the force back at Eve.

Finally, the attacks from Eve were no longer threatening. Not even painful. She had clearly lost what power she had gained from the black energy, and she had no way of getting any more inside the containment.

The woven spells, anchored by the rocks, were very strong, and getting stronger by the moment.

They had won.

Billie felt completely drained.

We have held her worst attacks.

Even Thomas was telling them they had all won. Billie could feel the excitement, the hope starting to build in all the others connected through Thomas.

Keep layering. Keep anchoring. Thomas's voice in her mind gave her power, gave her the strength to go on.

She did as she was told, as any good marine would do.

So did the others.

Billie could sense tiredness in everyone who touched her mind, but nothing could be allowed to escape from the prison they were building under the streets of New York. Not one thought, not one stray burst of energy.

Nothing.

Thomas anchored the reflective spell in stronger so that not even a remote-viewing spell would be possible from inside that sphere. At least not for hundreds of thousands of years.

Finally, Thomas told all of them to stop with a simple sentence.

We are finished.

Billie opened her eyes, blinking at the light in the Big Meeting Room. She was slouched in her chair, sweating. Her clothes stuck to her like wet bandages. She felt like a cab had backed up over her and parked on her head.

Beside her, Thomas somehow managed to push himself to his feet, clearly feeling the drain of energy as much as she did. He also had been sweating. Why did he always look so damned good while sweating?

Billie glanced around. Some of the people in the room looked like they might need medical attention. Ethti seemed even smaller, thinner, and more in need of a good meal than ever.

Thomas stepped up onto the stage and Ethti pushed herself to her feet and joined him.

"Thank you," Thomas said, "for your energy, your time, and your magic."

"Thank you for leading this fight," a woman near the back said.

A member of the council staggered to her feet and stepped up beside Thomas. "The council would like to officially thank everyone who helped."

Billie heard the words spoken aloud, as well as through a magic spell in her mind.

"And, as always, the council is in debt to Thomas."

She bowed to him.

A moment later, there were only the three of them left in the room.

Thomas and Ethti slumped down in chairs beside Billie while somehow Thomas remained standing.

"We won," Thomas said. "Eve is trapped forever."

"Are you sure?" Billie asked. "I'd hate to go through that again anytime soon."

Thomas nodded, clearly so tired that even a simple nod looked like work. "For the next year, every thirty seconds a different City Knight will wrap a new containment spell around Eve's cave, strengthening the spells that are there. She will live her remaining centuries out in that cave."

"With Payday Sam and a few hundred ancient hallows," Billie said. "With all the spells trapping her, she won't be able to get rid of them."

After a moment, all three of them laughed at the image. It was the laugh of the victors.

CHAPTER THIRTY-EIGHT

FORGOT SOMETHING

Billie stood in front of the large living-room window of her penthouse apartment and stared out over the city. The early-evening lights filled her view as far as she could see, their colors bright. It felt good to be home, even though this home had been hers for only just over a week. One of the longest weeks in recorded history, as far as she was concerned.

Her head still hurt from the fight with Eve, but a shower and a few aspirin had helped some. Now, in her thick, soft bathrobe, she planned on finding a snack and then dropping into bed for a long, long sleep.

Tomorrow was Halloween, the day Eve had scheduled to end the world. It looked like it was going to turn out to be just another holiday. All City Knights, no matter how tired, were scheduled to be on duty tomorrow afternoon and evening, since it was the most magically charged night of the year. It would be her first All Hallows' Eve as a City Knight, her first with knowledge not only that magic existed but that for some reason she had a lot of it.

And there was a part of that magic right now that was telling her to stay on guard. She didn't know why. Thomas had already checked a dozen times on Eve. Billie had even gone with him once or twice.

The feeling of warning continued.

Since she had gotten home, it had driven her nuts. Tomorrow she was going to have to talk to Thomas about ways of shutting off the magic at times. Right now she needed sleep.

"Still haven't figured it out yet?" a voice behind her said.

She spun around, holding her bathrobe closed.

A short, stubby man wearing a long stained apron and wiping his hands on a towel stood behind her. He had a sense of magic around him, yet unlike others, she couldn't see his magic, see how strong it was. And she couldn't tell if he was a Fantastic or not.

Under his apron he had on a brown pair of slacks and a white shirt with the sleeves rolled up. The apron looked as though it had been through a war zone, colored and stained with a dozen different things.

She had her privacy shields set at high around the apartment, and alarms should have triggered if anyone even tried to get in. He couldn't be standing there, yet he was.

"How did you get in here?"

He laughed, the sound dismissive. Then he moved into the kitchen area to the sink and began to wash his hands. "Corned beef. Let me tell ya, you never get the smell off. How people eat da stuff is beyond me."

"I personally like it," she said. "So, now that you've washed your hands, are you going to tell me who you are? And how you got past my shields?"

"Shields?" He glanced around, seemingly puzzled, then said, "Oh, *those* shields." He shook his head and used her hand towel to dry his hands, ignoring the well-used one he had draped over his shoulder. "You're good, but you could learn a thing or two."

"I didn't do those shields," she said. "I'm just a squire. I don't know how."

He shrugged. "That explains a lot." The guy took the towel off his shoulder, then removed his apron and tossed both over the back of a dining-area chair. Then he sat at the table, indicating that she should do the same across from him.

She started to say something snide about being invited to sit in her own home, then decided to just do as he said for now. At least until she figured out who he was.

The moment she sat and looked across the table into his eyes, she knew the answer. The eyes she saw were unicorn eyes, the same eyes that had been so huge in the Big Meeting Room in City Knights headquarters.

"So, I'm talking to the Last Great Unicorn King," Billie said. "Who, it seems, now works in a deli."

He smiled. "Off Broadway, in Midtown. And I don't work there, I own the place."

"*Now* I'm impressed," she said. "So to what do I owe the honor of this visit?"

He laughed. "You're quick, real quick. But if you're so smart, you tell me why I'm here."

Billie knew, even though she hadn't wanted to talk or even think about the possibility, and neither had any of the other City Knights. "Eve woke up Rallidae."

His face went serious as he nodded. "Almost. If the old birdbrain was really, fully awake, trust me, we'd all know it. But he's going to come around soon enough. I didn't think that stupid broad had the power to do it. I shoulda paid more attention. It was the ancient spell she was using. Unicorn blood and all."

He shook his head, clearly disgusted with Eve and more than likely disgusted with himself.

"So, from what I understand," Billie said, "you put Rallidae down there in the first place. Can't you just strengthen your original work and put him back to sleep?"

"Oh, sure, I put him there," the Great King said. He then made a snorting noise that sounded a little like laughter. "Me and about a hundred thousand of my soldiers, all working together."

"Oh," Billie said, not liking the sound of that at all.

"Yeah, 'oh' is right, sister," the Last Great Unicorn King said. "Rallidae is coming back up like a bad anchovy, and I can't think of a damn thing we can do about it."

CHAPTER THIRTY-NINE

CORNED BEEF ON A PLAN

"You hungry?" the Unicorn King asked Billie as they sat in silence at her dining-room table.

Billie nodded. Actually, she was.

"Good," he said. "I make the best damned corned-beef sandwich this side of the bridge."

"Which bridge?" she asked.

"Does it matter? Get dressed."

She nodded and magically changed her bathrobe to clean underwear, jeans, and a white blouse. Changing clothes was a very handy spell that Thomas had taught her early on, and she had practiced every day. "Ready."

He shook his head. "Fastest dresser of any human woman I have ever met."

"Not often I get offered corned beef," she said.

A moment later, the two of them were standing in the back hallway of a fairly busy deli. The moment she followed him into the main area, she recognized the place.

She was one block to the east off Broadway. She had eaten in here a hundred times, if not more.

This had been her favorite deli as a high school student, before she joined the Marines. This place had been her escape, her hole in the world to get away and be left alone. It had always felt safe, secure, for reasons she had never thought about.

Tonight, the place smelled of fresh pastrami, as it always did. The thirty-foot-long glass case separating the customers from the workers was filled with meats, salads, and a ton of desserts, including cinnamon rolls the size of basketballs.

Nothing appeared to have changed in her years in the Marines and then in Iraq.

She stared into the case, just as she had done when she was in school. She loved those cinnamon rolls. She used to buy one, then nibble on it for a few hours, sipping apple juice while sitting at a table watching the traffic and people go by outside.

The Last Great Unicorn King moved behind the counter, nodding to the two others who were working there. Now that he was behind the counter, and had his apron back on and the towel over his shoulder, she recognized him. He had always been there, a friendly, smiling face to a young girl in need of friendly, smiling faces.

He reached into an ice-filled display cooler and pulled out a bottled apple juice. He tossed it to her, and as she caught it he pointed to a table in the front corner. "Sit."

She stared at the bottle for a moment, then smiled at him. "Thanks."

How much did he know about her? Had he always been watching her? Had she come into this place because he had been here? So many questions.

But with Rallidae waking up at any moment, there just wasn't time to ask them.

She did as she was told, moving to the table and sitting, turning to watch the constant traffic outside the windows.

For a moment, she was a teenager again, sitting at this very same table, wondering if she was ever going to escape her foster parents, the city, and her awful high school. This table, and the tables to either side of it, had such an excellent sidewalk view. The location let her become part of the flow of the city without being out in it. For a half year or so, her dream while sitting at this very table had been to sit in an outdoor café in Paris.

She knew that with her new magic powers she could now jump to Paris in an instant if she wanted, but today protecting this table, this city seemed far more important to her.

The Great King slid the corned-beef sandwich in front of her, then sat down with a pastrami sandwich, digging in as if he hadn't eaten in a month.

She watched him for a moment, then did the same, not even coming close to getting her mouth around the wonderful-tasting meat and the soft rye bread.

After a few minutes, she stopped eating, took a drink of the juice, and then said, "Thanks. You're right, best corned beef this side of the bridge."

"And you doubted me why?" He wiped off his mouth with a napkin.

"So how long have you been watching me?" she asked.

"How old are you?"

"That long?"

"A moment only, in the grand scheme of things."

She smiled at him. For a sentence there, he had lost his Brooklyn accent and reverted to clear, formal English.

"What?" He wiped off his mouth again. "I say somethin' funny? Got a nose hair showing? What?"

"Just wondering why you are showing yourself to me, after all the years of staying hidden."

"I wasn't hidin'," he said. "I've been right back there for the past eighty years." He pointed to the counter.

"But making sure that none of your own people, or the City Knights, knew who you were. Right?"

He shrugged and kept eating.

"So why now, why me? I could still be a night watchman at Bloomingdale's if Ethti hadn't seen me."

Again, he gave his half laugh, half snort. "Nothin' happens by luck when it comes to magic."

"So why didn't you stop her yourself, before Eve went and woke up Rallidae?"

"I didn't know what she was doing, or even who was doin' what, until she had done it a half dozen times." He shook his head, pushing his sandwich away in disgust. "Stupid broad. What a fool. By the time I figured out where the ancient hallows were coming from, it was too late. Rallidae had already started to wake up. My original spell had been broken. And you City Knights were on the job stopping the woman, so I just let you do that, watching to make sure you succeeded."

"So why talk to me? My original question, remember?"

He shook his head. "What do they teach you in that Knights place?" He pointed out the window. "Look down the street. What do you see?"

She glanced in the direction he was pointing. "Cars, people, buildings."

"No, not your eyes. Look through your magic, then tell me what you see."

She stared at him for a moment, trying to decide if she should ask another question, then decided to try what he told her to try. Taking a deep breath, she closed her eyes and went down the staircase to the magic platform in her mind. Then, staying inside the magic, she opened her eyes and looked down the street.

Everyone seemed to be frozen in time, frozen in a moment.

She glanced around the deli. Everyone there was frozen except for the Great King sitting across from her.

"So you are looking at an instant in time, right? Now stare out at the street and imagine a week's worth of time passing."

She did as he instructed, running the people in fast-forward as if they were in a videotape. Suddenly everything was covered with a red mist, and instead of flesh-and-blood people walking the streets, it was skeletons.

Buildings collapsed, cars disappeared, and even more skeletons walked the streets. It was such a horrific vision that she didn't want to see any more. She closed her eyes and let her magic go.

"What is coming is as bad as I have ever seen. That's why I'm talking to you."

The Great King pulled his plate back toward him and took another bite of his sandwich.

She just felt sick. That was not a vision she was going to shake easily.

"So, do you know what part I'm going to play?" she asked.

"Nope," he said between chews.

"And no idea how to stop what's coming?"

"Not a clue, sister. A long time ago, when I was young and strong, we managed to put Rallidae down there before he took over the entire world and killed us all."

"Now he's coming back and you are no longer young, no longer strong, and no longer have an army."

"You got it," the Unicorn King said while wiping some loose pastrami from his mouth. "And this time Rallidae's going to be really pissed. Especially when he sees how we stripped all his bird people of their magic."

"So we can't let him see that. We can't let him wake up."

"Great idea," he said, shaking his head and taking another bite. "Wish I'd thought of it."

Chapter Forty

TIME FLIES WHEN YOU'RE REALLY OLD

Billie sat back, her stomach twisting, the idea of sleep and food no longer of interest to her. "Mind answering a few questions?" she asked.

He shrugged. "If you think it's gonna help."

"How did you trap Rallidae in the first place? How did you get him to sleep?"

The Great King shrugged. "In the big war, Rallidae was draining power from all his people, using it to defeat us. And we couldn't beat him. We were losing. My people, and other Fantastics fighting on our side, were being slaughtered."

"So what did you do?"

He smiled, clearly thinking back to the great victory as any soldier would. "We gave the flow of magic he was getting from his people a little push."

"You did what?"

He laughed. "We shoved him full of all his people's powers in one big burst. It drained every flying thing permanently of magic, and the overload short-circuited Rallidae in the process. Let me tell you, he hit hard when he landed, too. Came down from at least a mile up."

"And he's been out ever since?" Billie asked, shocked.

"No, not really." The Great King seemed embarrassed. "While he was knocked out, I turned him into a giant slug and put him in the cave below this island. Then I set up a dream spell in which he thought he was awake and ruling the world."

"So, all this time he's been dreaming, thinking he's been in charge?"

"You got it," he said, laughing. "But who's to say what's real and what isn't? Rallidae believed he was in charge, flying around ruling over the world and his people. He had beaten us in his dream state, so, for him, he was content and didn't want to break free of anything."

"Because he didn't know anything was holding him." Billie smiled at the elegant simplicity of the plan.

"That way a little regenerating sleep spell did the trick. A spell that would never normally hold him."

"But Eve broke that spell."

"Like a piece of china thrown against a brick wall. I've tried to fix it, rock him back to sleep like a big, stinking baby, but he's stirring. He knows when I'm close, knows something's wrong now, so it's only a matter of time before he wakes up."

"Will he stay in slug form?"

"Nope. He'll be flying again. And let me tell you, it's a sight. His wingspan can cover this island. Breaks all the laws of physics."

"So, without his people helping him with power, could you and your people beat him now?"

"No."

"Why not?" Billie asked, shocked at the immediacy and firmness of his answer.

"First off, we have fewer soldiers these days. It has been a long time since a unicorn has had to really fight. And we're all used to living lives as humans under the treaty. We've lost, or let go dormant, a lot of our powers. I was afraid of this, which was why I didn't back the treaty in the first place."

Billie nodded. "What's the other reason?"

"He has all the power of his people. We gave it to him when we knocked him out. When he wakes up, he's going to be a lot more powerful than the Rallidae I fought."

"Great," Billie said, slumping in the chair, not even daring to look out the window at the people and cars on the street. "And he's been sleeping for thousands of years. He's about as rested as they come."

"And he's going to be really, really angry."

They sat there in silence for a long few minutes.

"Can I see him? While he's still asleep?"

"Think it might help?"

"I have no idea."

"Neither do I, but it probably won't hurt to take a little peek. And I can tell you this much, after all these centuries, it's good to have someone to talk to about this."

Billie smiled.

The next instant a thick, ugly smell overwhelmed Billie as she and the Last Great Unicorn King were in a huge, dark cave. Thick, rich, the odor covered her like a heavy blanket, making it almost impossible to breathe.

She coughed a few times, the sound swallowed by the size of the cavern.

The Great King had a torch of some sort that flooded the place with a white light. Thousands and thousands of ancient hallows covered their eyes and cowered from the light in the rocks.

The center of the cave was filled with what looked like a long, giant mound of black gelatin. The skin on the thing looked translucent, with big blue veins pumping fluids through the mass. She couldn't tell which was the head end, and she doubted it made any difference.

As they watched, the big mound stirred and seemed to roll over, as if someone had turned over a big blob of gray, dirt-filled Jell-O. The waves of stinking flesh rolled over the rocks like waves over a pond. Hundreds of hallows screamed and scrambled for safety, their eyes still covered against the light.

"Seen enough?"

Billie nodded. "More than enough."

A moment later, she found herself back in her apartment. The Last Great Unicorn King stood a few feet away from her. "Take a shower, burn those clothes. I'll be back in fifteen minutes after I do the same thing."

Then he was gone.

A short while later, her hair still wet from a very hot shower, she sat across her dining-room table from the Last Great Unicorn King.

"What would happen if we put a big enough human-made bomb down there to blow him into a thousand pieces of goo?"

The Great King sat and stared into the distance, clearly thinking. Finally, he nodded. "It might work. But we would have to vaporize his body before his magical essence could escape and re-form. If we managed that, then he would be dead, as any of us would be."

"Good," Billie said.

"Of course, any bomb that could kill him might well carry enough charge to sink this whole island."

Billie hadn't thought of that. She must have been even more tired than she realized. She opened her mouth to make an alternative suggestion, but before she could even speak, the Unicorn King mumbled something about visiting an old customer who was a geologist. In a flash the King was gone.

Billie stared at the empty chair he had just occupied. She was going to have to ask him how he went through her security screens so easily. Maybe even learn a few spells from him, if they survived all this.

A huge if.

CHAPTER FORTY-ONE

PLAN B

The Last Great Unicorn King was going to have to work on his entrances. Here he was, the first Fantastic to get into City Knights headquarters in thousands of years, and he just popped in, no lights, no music, no smoke. Just a short deli owner in a dingy apron. Even so, Thomas and Ethti knew who he was immediately, and he had to wave off a lot of bowing and "an honor to meet you, sir"s.

Billie wanted to point to her wrist and say "Tick tock, folks," but decided a tactful clearing of the throat would go over better with her superiors. In the Marines, the worst they could do to a cocky recruit was throw her in the brig. She didn't even want to think about what the City Knights did to squires who got out of line.

"'Bout time you made some noise, kid," said the King. "My geologist buddy put the kibosh on your idea. He said a bomb would have taken out every borough of the city and maybe a coupla suburbs too." His

Brooklyn-shaped tones echoed in the Big Meeting Room. Billie tried to keep her voice steady as she reviewed the plan for Thomas and Ethti, who by the looks of it also had to try pretty hard—not to laugh.

"If the squire had reported to me earlier about your encounter, Your Highness, I might have saved you some time and effort."

Ouch, thought Billie. She was beginning to believe she would someday get a handle on this whole magic thing, but it was clear that protocol would always be beyond her.

"Yes, even if there were minimal risk of civilian casualties, a human-made bomb could never have worked. Even the smallest parts of Rallidae's body would have held his essence, enough to allow him to re-form," Thomas said. "Not that we don't appreciate the . . . creative suggestion, Squire."

Not that I don't appreciate the backhanded compliment, Thomas. God, it was annoying how attractive he was, even in smug mode.

As the two experienced City Knights discussed other options with the ancient and powerful king, Billie began to feel smaller and smaller. She had learned so much in the past week, but she still didn't know anywhere near enough to even help work on the problem.

Why was she bothering? The money and perks of this job were nice, to be sure, but Billie would never earn these people's respect; she was just magical muscle to them and would never be anything more. It was frustrating as hell, and almost made her understand how someone like Eve could turn evil. Not that Billie would ever do that, of course. Once you started thinking like Eve, there was no turning back.

Once you started thinking like Eve . . .

"Maybe Eve had the right idea," Billie blurted out before she could stop herself. Yep, had to work on that protocol.

"You think Eve had the right idea waking this monster up?" the Unicorn King echoed incredulously. Thomas and Ethti just stared at her. Big as the Big Meeting Room was, it was starting to feel awfully stuffy, and close.

"Not waking him up," Billie said, tugging at her suddenly too-tight collar. "Draining his power. She wasn't doing it very well, and for the wrong reasons, not to mention the barbaric, ancient spell she used. But she had the right idea."

The silence in the big room was intense. Billie was afraid for a moment that she had suddenly lost all her hearing. The Great King stared off into space.

Thomas paced.

Ethti had turned and had her back to everyone.

"It might be possible," Ethti finally said, turning to face the Great King.

"What would you suggest doing with all the black energy and power?" said the Great King.

"Give it back to his people," Billie said. "From what you have told me, he got a great deal of the power *from* his people. And you knocked him out using that power. We drain the power out of him and give it back, only in very small amounts per bird."

"You know how many billions of birds there are now on this planet?" the King said.

"That's why it would work," Billie said.

"The squire has an interesting idea," Ethti said, nodding.

Thomas kept pacing.

"So," the Great King said. "I see two problems. First, you need to create a linked spell with enough magic creatures to be powerful enough to drain that much energy without being affected by it."

"And?" Thomas asked when the Great King stopped for a moment to think.

"Then you have to spread the power out to the birds of the planet." He stared at Billie. "I think the second problem might have a solution."

Billie ignored his look and comment and focused on the first problem. "Link your people," Billie said. "I know you can do it, because I did it."

"And we could get the other Fantastic leaders to help," Ethti said.

"No," the Great King said. "The young one is right. It would have to be my people. We are the only ones who would not be harmed by Rallidae's power and darkness."

"Would they do that?" Thomas asked. "All of them?"

The Great King laughed. "Of course they would. I'm their king. I'll be back. You figure out how to deal with the second problem of getting Rallidae's energy to his people. Let me deal with extracting it."

And with that, the Last Great Unicorn King was gone.

CHAPTER FORTY-TWO

TALKING TO THE PIGEONS IN THE PARK

They came up with nothing. They couldn't come up with one stinking spell, in Billie's magic room or even in the library, that could link birds who didn't have magic in their systems already, or any creatures without magic for that matter.

Without a way to break up and distribute the black energy being taken from Rallidae, Thomas was sure he would re-form.

"Maybe we're going about this wrong," Thomas said. "Maybe we don't need a link to get the energy to the entire population of birds on the planet."

"Not following, I'm afraid."

"Look," Thomas said, pacing on the stage in the Big Meeting Room, "we know the energy can be dispersed easily, because Eve did it to spread out the sprites."

Suddenly, Billie saw where he was heading. "If we disperse the energy evenly over the entire planet, all we need to do is put something with the energy that would attract it to birds only."

"Exactly," Thomas said. "And I think I know of an attraction spell that just might do that. Used for lovers, but it should work with some minor changes."

"A love-potion spell?"

"It might work," Ethti said. "We have to set it for birds and charge every particle of Rallidae energy released with it."

"With what?" the Great King asked as he appeared next to Billie. She and Thomas explained the plan.

The King nodded in agreement. "Yeah, with just about every unicorn in the world working at the same time, we can draw about a thousand different streams of energy from Rallidae at the same time and scatter it into the air. That should drain the old monster before he even has a chance to wake up and fight back. Then we drop the roof of the cave on what's left of his slug body."

"And the City Knights can charge the energy as the streams pass with the love-potion spell to attract it only to birds," Thomas said.

The Great King looked at Billie. "There's only one problem I can see. We need you to link us all together."

"You can't do it?" she asked.

He laughed. "Oh, sure I could. And so could a number of my council. But we're going to be a little busy sucking that big slug dry. You can link us all, keep us working together at the exact same moment."

"Why the squire?" Ethti asked. "We have many City Knights far more experienced than she is."

Billie felt a wave of panic threatening to send her running. She forced herself to take a deep breath and dig down into her Marine training again. Marines never ran. They faced the task.

"It's not experience I'm after," the Great King said.

Ethti smiled ever so slightly. Thomas just looked away.

Billie was confused. What the hell was he implying with that "experience" crack? Okay, so she hadn't been on the job for long, but it wasn't as if she had never . . . oh. Come to think of it, she *had* never . . . She had joined the Marines at seventeen, and that kept her too busy for much of a social life, and so she had never . . .

Virgins and unicorns. Right.

"Ethti is right," she said, speaking far too quickly. "The last time I linked all your people, it was only for a light alarm spell."

"And you did it in less than a minute," the Great King said. "I'll help you set up the contact. I'll tell all my people what you are going to do, so they will help you instead of fight you. But then my full attention must be on the spells, not on the communication with my people."

"You think I can do this?"

"These two, and all the rest of the powerful City Knights, will be standing right with you. Right?"

Thomas nodded.

The Great King laughed, merrily and without innuendo, and Billie suddenly remembered that laugh from all the times in school she had been in his deli. All the big smiles he had given her, the winks, the extra helpings. He had been watching her most of her life. If he suggested she do something, he knew she could do it.

So before he could stop laughing and answer, she said, "When do we start?"

"We start when you people get your act together. You're going to need just about every City Knight on the planet to be love-potion-spelling the thousands of energy streams coming up from Rallidae's cave. And you're going to need a whole bunch of cover stories for all the people in the city who see the energy streams."

"Give us two hours," Thomas said.

"Not a moment longer," the Great King said. "Right back here."

With a wink at Billie, he vanished.

"Oh, crap, what have I gotten myself into?" Billie said, barely holding the panic down. She couldn't talk to and coordinate every unicorn on the planet at the same time. Hell, up until a week ago she didn't even believe unicorns existed.

"Saving the world," Thomas said. "You signed on to help save the world. That's what the City Knights do, one magic spell at a time."

"Someone should put that on a sign over the recruitment door."

"You mean it's not there?" Thomas asked with a twinkle in his eye.

"Not when I came in," Billie said, managing a tiny smile herself.

"I'll have that fixed at once," Thomas said. Then he touched her arm, holding it gently. "You'll do fine."

CHAPTER FORTY-THREE

BAREBACK AND LOVING IT

Billie started down her now-familiar magic staircase fully expecting to end up in her now-familiar magic basement. Instead she found herself standing in an open field full of short green grass and bright sunshine.

Beside her stood an eight-foot-tall creature with a white coat that shimmered in the sunlight. He was built like a horse except for his massive, swirling eyes and the colorful and *extremely* long horn on his forehead. He had a long white beard, a long white mane and tail, and cloven hooves.

"Wow," she said.

"Like the look?" asked the Unicorn King.

"You are really spectacular."

"I know. Now, you want to get on with it, or are you just gonna gawk all day?"

"I'm up for gawking, actually," she said, smiling at him.

"Later, kid. Later. We have work to do. Now climb on board and let's see if we can build this link."

"Climb on?" she asked. She stared at the creature in front of her. She had ridden in tanks, troop transports, and Humvees. But never, in all her years growing up in New York City, had she ever ridden a horse, let alone a giant unicorn.

"Just imagine yourself on my back," he said. "Remember, we're in your magic."

"I won't hurt you?" she asked.

For a moment, she was worried that he would never stop laughing.

CHAPTER FORTY-FOUR

HUMANS GET NO RESPECT

Riding on the Unicorn King's back was like no experience Billie could ever have imagined. The Great King's power radiated up through her body, giving her confidence. She never once felt in danger of falling.

They jumped from one of his people to the next. At first Billie needed the Great King's help in linking his people into her remote-viewing spell, but then it became easier and easier, faster and faster, until she felt they couldn't move any faster.

Yet, somehow, they did.

And somehow, even as each new unicorn was added to the network, she could still keep track of all the others.

Finally she found herself standing in front of ten unicorns, all facing her and the Great King in a semicircle in an open field of green grass. As she and the Great King approached, he said, "This is where you get off, kid."

She slid off and walked the final twenty paces to the unicorns beside him.

They were all far larger than any horses she had ever seen, but none were as big as the Great King. All had the fantastic swirling eyes full of rainbows of color. All had horns that looked far too long for their heads. It was the most incredible sight she had ever seen.

"It is a sad day when our Great King walks with a human as an equal," the unicorn in the center said.

She knew instantly, from her links with all the unicorns, that his name was Tagar, and he was the Great King's second-in-command and leader of the Great Unicorn Council. She also knew that there had been bad blood between them for centuries, made worse when the Great King would not lead his people to sure death in a final battle against the expanding human hordes. With two others siding with him on the council, Tagar had never taken human form. Instead he had lived in remote areas and relied on magic to go unseen for centuries.

"Our people and the humans are working together to stop Rallidae," the Great King said, his voice a rich, musical sound in Billie's head. A lovely sound, indeed, but some small part of Billie, deep down inside, missed the Brooklyn accent.

"A human caused the problem," Tagar said.

"Rallidae would have awoken in the next few hundred years without the human. But we need them to solve this."

"Again, we are only putting off the final battle," Tagar said, disgusted. "He will re-form, again with his army behind him, given enough centuries."

"And we will prepare for such a return," the Great King said. "And unite all the Fantastics against him, and along with our human friends we will win."

Billie could not take it any longer. "Excuse me, but you talk as if we've already won this battle. We have not. I was taught you always take one fight, one battle, at a time. Win enough battles and the war is yours."

"The human is correct," another unicorn, near the end of the semicircle, said.

Billie instantly, from her links, knew his name. Campderees, a supporter of the King and the oldest known unicorn still left alive. All the unicorns on her link were amazed that he had spoken. And awed. He had not spoken to his people, or at a Great Council meeting, since the Great King rejected the human-Fantastic treaty.

Billie could feel the emotions of an entire race as they dropped in behind the Great King and Campderees.

Tagar stared at the Great King, then bowed his head slightly, not allowing his horn to reach level and point at the Great King, which Billie knew would have been a challenge instead of a nod of honor.

"Lead us," Tagar said, "and we will follow."

A sigh of relief went through the entire unicorn population.

Campderees nodded to Billie. "Humans have grown, as we knew they would. Impressive."

"So join the link and let us spread Rallidae's power, his essence, to his people, where it cannot harm us for centuries to come."

Quickly, starting on the left, Billie added in the council, their minds and magic bolstering immeasurably the power of the link.

"Good," the Great King said. "Now link with me, and we will be ready to start."

Billie took a deep breath and did as instructed, letting the magic of the Great King join the link with his people. She could feel the awe and respect from all of them, including Tagar. It seemed that over the centuries they had forgotten the reason he was known only as the Great King. After this, they would remember again for centuries.

"We are linked," the Great King said.

Billie watched, remaining silent, as he checked with Thomas.

"The humans are ready. Billie, direct us."

A moment later, she found herself standing on a ledge in Rallidae's cave, staring down through the dark at the giant slug. Since her actual body still sat in the Big Meeting Room in City Knights headquarters, she didn't bother to turn on the smell feature.

She adjusted her vision so that she could see perfectly in the darkness. Then she made one final adjustment to her vision. She marked the essence of Rallidae as a bright blue light. It filled the cave, almost blinding her with its power.

Until that blue light was completely extinguished, they could not stop.

Through the link, she could sense the three hundred different teams aiming their spells at Rallidae. She directed each spell to a specific place on the great slug until the entire thing was covered.

She took a deep breath.

"Now."

A moment later, Rallidae let out a massive scream of pain as three hundred round suction spells started to drain his energy, sending it through the ceiling and out to the birds of the world in giant columns of blackness.

Rallidae rolled over, trying to get away from the spells, but Billie adjusted the aim of all the teams of unicorns, having each move its spell to an exact location, keeping Rallidae's entire body covered at all times, no matter how much he moved.

Ancient hallows were being smashed and killed by the hundreds as they struggled to stay out of the great creature's way.

Again, Rallidae screamed in pain. This time it sounded more birdlike.

An image of an immense bird rose up over New York, towering into the night sky like a huge monster, trying to escape.

Billie focused all her will and might on keeping the unicorn teams on target, draining the great slug creature of its energy.

Again Rallidae screamed and again she could see what he had been thousands of years before, a huge, impressive creature with a razor-sharp beak and a wingspan of miles.

His feathers were the colors of the rainbow, his eyes dark, the size of Yankee Stadium.

With every twist and turn of the slug-shaped Rallidae, she had to adjust dozens of spells to different locations, keeping him covered like a blanket.

And she had to ignore his phantom image.

Then she noticed that he was getting smaller. There was more overlap in the areas of the spells.

"We are winning," she sent through the link. "He is shrinking. *Do not stop.*"

But the smaller he became, the closer he got to waking up completely, to becoming more mobile.

His image flapped its wings, smashing buildings along the shoreline of the Hudson, knocking tops off three buildings.

In the cave, his slug form thrashed around, trying to get away from the intense pain of his energy.

Billie stayed with him, kept the spells spot on target, never letting an instant go by with even an inch of him not covered by a draining spell or two.

"Who dares attack Rallidae?" a voice echoed through the cave and around inside Billie's mind.

Again she saw his huge image.

For an instant she thought she had lost the link with the unicorns, but she hadn't. But every unicorn along the link had heard the voice.

And every City Knight on the surface.

And everyone had seen the fantastic image of the huge bird struggling over the city.

No one faltered, no one stopped.

Billie kept the spells directed on the fighting slug thrashing around in the cave. It was visibly smaller, and the bright blue light was starting to dim.

"I demand to know who attacks me!" Rallidae shouted, the voice inside and outside of Billie's head.

Rallidae had lost enough mass that now most of the spells tracking him were doubling up, taking his energy twice as fast.

"I do," Billie projected toward the creature being sucked dry on the floor of the cave. "I am giving back to your people what you took from them."

"They were my people," Rallidae said, his voice clearly weaker, less powerful. "I am their leader. I have the right to take from them what I want."

"It doesn't work that way in the world anymore," Billie told the Bird King. "Sorry."

The blue light dimmed even more.

"Do not stop!" Billie shouted to the link as some unicorn teams started to falter.

She directed the stronger teams to the center of the much smaller Rallidae, then had the weaker teams overlap, shifting hundreds of draining spells around at the same time.

But she was growing tired, having more trouble holding the link together.

Rallidae's body was now the size of a dozen semitrailers and trucks, and shrinking by the moment. The blue light was only a faint shadow of what it had been in the beginning.

But it was still there.

"We're not finished yet," she told the unicorns over the link. "We can't stop until he is completely spread out over the world."

"Humans?" Rallidae asked, his voice now shallow and sounding hollow in Billie's head.

"The Great King?"

Billie kept the spells on target and ignored Rallidae's voice.

"How is this possible? I defeated you centuries ago. I never allowed the humans to breed."

"Seems it was all a dream," Billie told Rallidae.

In her mind, she could hear the Great King laughing. And his laugh energized her and the rest of his people to keep going.

Under the onslaught of three hundred draining spells, Rallidae shrank visibly every second, forcing Billie to move faster and faster to keep the spells on their target.

She could feel the strain eating at her mind, at her very soul, but she wouldn't stop.

Quitting now was not an option.

"I will return," Rallidae said, his voice now a whisper in her head and along the link to the other unicorns.

"And we will be waiting," Billie said as the last of Rallidae shrank down so that the area under ten spells covered him, then five, then just one as all three hundred draining spells took the last of him out of the cave and spread him over the world.

"Stay with me," Billie said to the unicorns as she searched the cave for any remaining blue light. "I want to run the draining spells over every inch of this cave, just to be safe."

"Hurry," the Great King said back to her. "Many of my people cannot hold on much longer."

She wondered if he knew that she was barely holding on as it was.

Billie directed the three hundred spells to cover the cave like three hundred ends of a vacuum-cleaner hose, sucking up anything left of Rallidae that might have been hiding in a corner, left on an ancient sprite, or just sloughed off by the giant slug.

Finally the last area of the cave was covered.

No blue light remained, even in the faintest glimmering.

"We are finished."

"Thank you," the Great King said over the link a moment before Billie broke it. "We have won this battle. For the second time, Rallidae has been defeated."

Billie was alone in her own mind.

She could feel the relief flooding through her as if a dam had broken. They had won. The world would continue, for a time anyway.

She dropped down to her knees and tried to catch her breath as she took one last look around the cave. She never wanted to see this place again.

Then, just as she felt she would pass out from the exhaustion, she tried to return to her body in the City Knights headquarters.

Nothing.

"Man, I must be real tired," she said out loud.

A nearby hallow stared at her, then pointed, snickering.

The hallows shouldn't have been able to see her. They didn't have the right kind of magic.

One reached up and touched her.

Apalled, she knocked its filthy hand away, then stepped back as the stench of the place hit her.

Her entire body was here, in the cave, with the hallows.

How could that have happened? She had been in the Big Meeting Room when she left with the Great King. Had he transported her down here to make sure she did a good job?

She summoned what strength she had left and tried to spell herself out of the cave. She was stopped by a very strong containment spell. It felt as if she had run into a wall at full walk.

She moaned and tried to stand, finally giving up and just lying down against a rock.

A mirror spell, much like the one they had set up around Eve's cavern, was linked with the containment spell. She couldn't even get a remote-viewing spell out of the cave.

Even exhausted as she felt, she could tell that the spell was as strong as, if not stronger than, the one they had set up against Eve.

Was it left over from Rallidae's imprisonment?

She didn't think so. He would have been able to break through it easily. There would have been no point, and she would have noticed it on her first visit here.

Had he set it up as a last-minute attack against her? Possible. She was so new at magic, she *didn't know* a thousand times more than she knew.

She slapped another hallow away, then set up a shield around herself to keep them and most of the smell out.

All she wanted to do was close her eyes, to sleep, to just let go and forget everything.

It appeared that they had won a very large battle. But she, personally, had another one to fight.

And she just didn't have any energy left.

She let her eyes close. Maybe a little rest and she would be able to find her way out. After all, she had worked hard, fought hard, held an entire army of unicorns together with her mind. She deserved the rest.

Just a few minutes of sleep.

What could it hurt?

CHAPTER FORTY-FIVE

DIDN'T KNOW THAT

Thomas jumped back to the Big Meeting Room the moment the victory signal had been given and the energy streams had shut off. He wanted to be there to congratulate Billie and to help her through the post-magic-stress issues she was sure to face.

Her mind had been stretched farther than any new recruit's had ever been stretched. She had been asked to perform spells she was not used to. She was going to need some help to put everything in her magic back in order, and about a week's worth of sleep and good food on top of that.

After what she had just done, Thomas considered it his duty, and pleasure, to make sure his squire was taken care of. Without her, he doubted the unicorns could have pulled off what they did. Besides that, there hadn't been a woman in decades that had interested him the way Billie did. Spending time with her would be a joy on that side as well, no matter how tired she might be.

The Great King had already left, leaving Billie the only one in the room, slumped in her chair.

Ethti appeared a moment later, and they both moved to where Billie slouched, her eyes still closed.

Thomas sat on one side of her, Ethti on the other.

"Billie?" Thomas said, his voice as gentle as he could make it. "Come on back. It's over."

He moved to touch her, but she slapped his hand away, not opening her eyes.

Then, suddenly, it looked as if she was smelling something very sour.

"Billie," he said, his voice a little more forceful. "Come on back. It's over."

Ethti stared at Billie for a moment. Thomas could tell that Ethti was gently probing at Billie's mind, trying to see what was happening.

After a moment, Ethti shook her head. "She's still in the cave. She thinks she's trapped by a containment and mirror spell."

Thomas had gone to touch Billie again on the shoulder when suddenly Billie put up a protection screen, pushing both Thomas and Ethti away.

"She thinks we're hallows," Ethti said.

Then Billie slumped to the floor and curled up as if she were going to sleep.

"No! Billie!" Thomas shouted.

If she went to sleep in her magic, at this level of exhaustion, she might never return. He had seen it happen a number of times to recruits who had overreached themselves and the levels of their own skills. The magic held them inside, trapped forever in a vegetative state.

Ethti stood, took a deep breath, and aimed a high-energy probe at Billie's protect spell. Thomas could tell that it was one designed to cause pain as well as cut through the barrier.

Billie stirred and moaned, but the barrier didn't break.

"She is very powerful," Ethti said.

Thomas felt a level of panic rising in his stomach. They couldn't lose Billie now. Not after having her with them for only a short week.

He thought about trying to break through her screens as well, but knew he couldn't. He had trained her; he knew how powerful she was, even without any training. And that was before the events of the last day or so.

They needed help and they needed it quickly.

With every ounce of energy he had left, he broadcast a call for help to the Last Great Unicorn King.

Billie is in danger. We need your help!

A moment later, the Great King and the most ancient of all unicorns, Campderees, appeared. The Great King wore his deli apron and smelled like pastrami.

Campderees appeared as a teenage boy in a T-shirt and jeans, with tattoos and a nose ring.

The Great King strode over close to Billie, then stared at her. "Too tired to get home, huh?"

The Great King shook his head. "I forgot how new she was to her magic."

The Great King sat down in a chair and nodded to Thomas. "Excuse me while I go fetch her."

He closed his eyes, and the deli owner's body the Great King used as a disguise relaxed into the chair and then vanished.

"I hope he gets there in time," Campderees said, clearly worried. "I will monitor his progress." He sat down and closed his eyes.

Thomas stared at the oldest living unicorn. If someone with that much power and knowledge was worried, this was bad.

Very bad.

CHAPTER FORTY-SIX

ATTENTION

"**H**ey, sister. No sleepin' on da job."

Billie stirred, the voice seeming to be a long way away. She should know the voice, but she couldn't quite place it. It didn't matter. All she wanted to do was get some sleep.

The voice called out a few more times. She was about to tell the voice to come back in ten hours, but then it seemed to fade into the distance as she started to doze off.

Suddenly there was the sound of RPG fire near her, with bombs exploding in the distance. She could smell the gunpowder and then see even through her closed eyes the bright flashes of gunfire in the darkness.

"Marine! Attention!"

The voice of her CO in Iraq echoed through her head.

She sprang to her feet. A feeling of dizziness shot through her, but she fought to remain on her feet and at attention at all costs.

"Sleeping on duty, marine?"

The voice came from behind her.

More firing, more explosions nearby. She must be close to a pretty good mixer.

She tried blinking her eyes, focusing them on the darkness in front of her, letting the dizziness go away from the sudden movement.

"Sir. Just resting, sir!"

Her voice echoed in the cave.

Rallidae's cave.

Wait. She was still in Rallidae's cave, with the thousands of ancient hallows. She was having a hallucination. She wasn't in Iraq. She was still trapped and tired beyond words.

She started to move, to sit down again, to close her eyes and go to sleep.

More RPG fire, more explosions, only this time closer. The ground shook under her, as it had many times in Iraq, over many a night. Dust clogged the air.

"Did I give you permission to move, marine?"

By instinct, she snapped back to attention. "Sir. No sir."

Again, her voice echoed in the cave. She could see it clearly around her. Rallidae's cave. She could see hallows, the area where Rallidae had slept for centuries.

How was this possible?

How did her CO get behind her in the cave? It had to be a hallucination, but she was so exhausted, she didn't dare challenge it.

"Your duty, soldier," her CO said, staying behind her back, "is to get back to City Knights headquarters on the double. No sleeping or resting allowed."

"Sir? I am—"

"No excuses, marine. Marines don't make excuses; they get the job done."

"Sir. Yes, sir."

"Now move it! I'll back you up."

She focused all her strength, all her magic, on returning to the Big Meeting Room. At first, the energy it took to break through the containment and mirror barriers seemed like it would be too much for her tired mind and body.

But then she saw a weak spot, an opening, and without waiting an instant, she went through it and returned to the Big Meeting Room.

She opened her eyes to see the worried looks of Thomas and Ethti. Before she realized what she had done, she snapped to her feet, standing at attention.

"Reporting as ordered."

The movement was too much, even for a trained marine. She toppled forward and Thomas caught her before she hit the ground face-first.

He eased her over on her back in his arms and smiled, the most wonderful smile she had seen in what seemed to be aeons.

"You're back. You're safe."

She nodded, afraid to speak. What the heck had just happened?

Thomas glanced up at a smiling Last Great Unicorn King. "What did you do?"

He laughed, a laugh that sounded wonderful to Billie. "Just used a little of her own training to help her along."

She felt stunned at just how close she had come to being lost in her own magic forever. It seemed she needed a lot more time on Thomas's couch in training sessions before she would get this magic stuff even slightly under control.

"Thanks for coming and getting me," she said, smiling at the Great King.

He smiled and leaned down. "It is you we owe the thanks to. I'm not sure I would have been able to do what you did down there against Rallidae."

"Yeah, right," she laughed. No wonder his deli was always packed. The Last Great Unicorn King really knew how to flatter a customer.

The Great King laughed with her. "Gotta admit, it sounded good."

"It did," she said, smiling. "And I appreciate it. Very nice of you to say in front of my friends."

"It was, wasn't it?" he said, smiling at Thomas, then winking at Ethti.

Then he looked down at Billie with his large, swirling eyes full of color. "Come on by for a corned beef when ya get rested." He nodded in the direction of Thomas. "Bring a date."

With that, the Last Great Unicorn King was gone.

CHAPTER FORTY-SEVEN

CAN'T MISS THE FIRST ONE

Halloween. The most magic-filled night of the year.

Every City Knight would be on duty except her. Thomas and Ethti had given her the night off, to rest.

Well, screw that, she didn't need the night off.

She tossed the covers back and climbed out of bed, surprised that she was nude. How had Thomas gotten her in bed? She tried to remember. Had he undressed her?

Then she remembered that a few hours ago, after he had come back to feed her some lunch, she had undressed herself and crawled back into bed, without him watching. She wouldn't have minded him seeing her without clothes on. But she hoped, when that time came, it would be under other circumstances. And that she had enough energy to remember it.

Fifteen minutes later, she was showered, dressed, and heading down the elevator to the street. She'd nab some coffee and a bagel at the deli across the street, then take a cab to the meeting.

On the way down the elevator, she did a quick check by remote viewing to make sure Eve was still securely locked into place.

She was.

Billie would give almost anything to see how Eve was faring inside that containment field with the hallows and a mass murderer for company. But no one dared look for fear of releasing her. Maybe in a few hundred years, when any power she might have had would be drained, someone could take a peek.

Five minutes before the meeting was scheduled to start, Billie walked into the Big Meeting Room, coffee and bagel in hand, and took a seat next to her surprised partner, Thomas.

"I'm glad you're here and doing well," Thomas said. "But I'm going to force you to take it easy this evening. No magic, understood?"

"Understood," she said.

The next moment, Ethti appeared on the raised area at the front of the big room. She immediately saw Billie sitting there and frowned.

The City Knights' newest recruit raised her coffee cup to her boss, then shook her head, indicating that Ethti should ignore her and just go on.

You should be sleeping.

The petite woman's thought was clear in her mind.

I know, she thought back. *But I couldn't miss my first Halloween night. I'll take it easy, stay with Thomas, go home early. Thomas made me promise no magic.*

I'm going to hold you to that.

I hope so.

Ethti nodded.

Then she started the meeting, going over the problems the city might face tonight. Roving bands of humans were the least of their worries. For some reason, tonight many Fantastics thought they could shed their human skins and just play freely, treaty or no treaty. Trolls and elves were the worst, although at times brownies, goblins, and nymphs caused their share of mischief.

Ethti spent the next ten minutes going over a few standard cover stories to spell humans who had seen Fantastics.

Billie listened carefully to everything. She just wanted to be here with the other City Knights and do her job. She could learn a lot on a night like this and it was clear she still had a lot to learn. Luckily, she had a lot of time to learn it, if she didn't do anything stupid over the next few thousand years.

Or tonight, for that matter.

"Assignments," Ethti said, starting down the list.

When she got to Thomas's name, she said, "Thomas, you and your squire will be in Midtown, along Broadway. Stay alert for a band of goblins coming up out of the subway in that area. They may have wolves with them."

Billie knew, right at that moment, that coming to the meeting had been the right thing for her. The pressure she had felt over the past few days was melting. It would be good for her, good for her peace of mind, to just do her job and work to become a full City Knight, a member of the Soldats de la Fantastiques.

Besides, even with the risks, this was simply a great job. She got to meet interesting people and creatures, do fun and challenging tasks, and save the world.

Plus, in what other job could you ride on the back of a giant unicorn? Maybe there were some advantages to being a virgin.

You still think you're a virgin?

The Last Great Unicorn King's voice echoed in her head.

She laughed, causing Thomas to glance at her.

I am. Honest.

Yeah, and what about that Stan kid when you were a junior in high school?

Hey, not funny. That didn't count.

Sure it didn't. His laugh echoed through her mind. *Stop by for a sandwich later anyway. I hear you're gonna be in da neighborhood.*

She promised she would, and ten minutes later she and Thomas were headed out of the City Knights headquarters for a night patrolling the streets on the most magic-filled night of the year.

Her first Halloween. She had no doubt that this would be one she would remember.

ABOUT THE AUTHOR

Bestselling author, editor, and World Fantasy Award winner Dean Wesley Smith has written more than seventy popular novels, both his own and tie-in projects, including *Laying the Music to Rest* and *X-Men: The Jewels of Cyttorak*. With Kristine Kathryn Rusch he is the coauthor of The Tenth Planet trilogy and the motion picture novelization *X-Men*, along with more than a dozen Star Trek books and two original Men in Black novels. He has also written novels in a number of gaming universes, including Vor, Final Fantasy, and the novelization for the movie *Final Fantasy*.

REALMS OF FANTASY

The largest magazine in the world devoted to fantasy.

Think of things dark and things dangerous.
Of magical lands and mysterious creatures.
Of heroic quests. Summoned spirits.
Sorcery and swordplay. Talismans and dragons...

FREE TRIAL ISSUE

CALL 1-800-219-1187 TO RECEIVE YOUR FREE ISSUE
Or use the coupon below to order by mail

Please send me a FREE TRIAL ISSUE of Realms of Fantasy magazine. If I like it I will receive 5 more issues. If I choose not to subscribe, I will return the bill marked "cancel" and keep the FREE trial issue. Otherwise I'll return the invoice with payment of $16.95 ($21.95 international).

AD0305

Name_____

Address_____

City_____ State_____ Zip_____

Mail To: Sovereign Media 30 W. Third Street, Third Floor, Williamsport, PA 17701

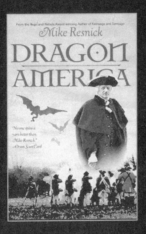

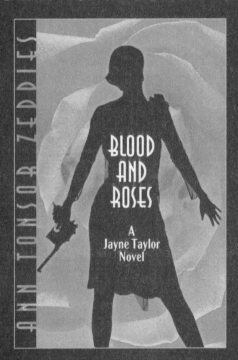

ALSO FROM PHOBOS BOOKS . . .

Empire of Dreams and Miracles
Edited by Orson Scott Card
and Keith Olexa
ISBN: 0-9720026-0-X
"...every story in Empire of Dreams
and Miracles *is a masterpiece!"*
—Alex Black

Hitting the Skids in Pixeltown
Edited by Orson Scott Card
and Keith Olexa
ISBN: 0-9720026-0-X
"Mind-expanding quality stories.
Hitting The Skids In Pixeltown *is
enthusiastically recommended to
every dedicated fan of science fiction."*
—Midwest Book Review

All the Rage This Year
Edited by Keith Olexa
ISBN: 0-9720026-5-0
*"*All the Rage This Year *is an excellent
anthology of stories that will surprise,
and possibly even shock, readers."*
—Book Nook

Absolutely Brilliant in Chrome
Edited by Keith Olexa
ISBN: 0-9720026-3-4
*"Each story is a gem, perfect, polished,
illuminating."*
—Wigglefish.com

Nobody Gets the Girl
James Maxey
ISBN: 0-9720026-2-6
*"[A] clever book — the pace never flags . . .
it's hard to put the book down."*
— The SF Site

Counterfeit Kings
Adam Connell
ISBN: 0-9720026-4-2
*"Struggle for identity and self-sacrifice
are just a few of the powerful stories beneath
an action-packed surface plot that provokes
as it dazzles."* —Publishers Weekly

PHOBOS IMPACT . . . IMPACTING THE IMAGINATION

PHOBOS IMPACT
An Imprint of Phobos Books LLC, 200 Park Ave South, New York, NY 10003
Voice: 347-683-8151 Fax: 718-228-3597
Distributed to the trade by National Book Network 1-800-462-6240

PHOBOS IMPACT

An Imprint of Phobos Books LLC. 200 Park Ave South, New York, NY 10003
Voice: 347-683-8151 Fax: 718-228-3597
Distributed to the trade by National Book Network 1-800-462-6240

Sandra Schulberg
Publisher

John J. Ordover
Editor-in-Chief

Kathleen David
Associate Editor

Matt Galemmo
Art Director

Terry McGarry
Production Editor

Julie Kirsch
Production Co-ordinator

Andy Heidel
Marketing Director

Keith Olexa
Webmaster

Chris Erkmann
Advertising Associate